BAHIA
BLUES

Yasmina Traboulsi was born in 1975. She worked as a lawyer before writing *Bahia Blues*, for which she won the Young Francophone Writer's Award in 2002, and the Prix du Premier Roman in 2003. She lives in London.

Polly McLean is a freelance translator based in Oxford. Her recent work includes *Secret* by Philippe Grimbert (Portobello Books) and Catherine Deneuve's *Close Up and Personal* (Weidenfeld & Nicholson).

YASMINA TRABOULSI

BAHIA BLUES

Translated by Polly McLean

Arcadia Books Ltd
15–16 Nassau Street
London WIW 7AB

www.arcadiabooks.co.uk

First published in the United Kingdom by BlackAmber, an imprint of Arcadia Books 2007
Originally published by Mercure de France as *Les enfants de La Place* 2003
Copyright © Yasmina Traboulsi 2003

This English translation from the French
Copyright © Polly McLean 2007

Yasmina Traboulsi has asserted her moral right to be identified as the author of this work
in accordance with the Copyright, Designs and Patents Act, 1988.

A catalogue record for this book is available from the British Library.

ISBN 1-905147-28-7

Designed and typeset in Galliard by Discript Limited, London WC2N 4BN
Printed in Finland by WS Bookwell

This book is supported by the French Ministry for Foreign Affairs, as part of
the Burgess programme headed for the French Embassy in London by the
Institut Français du Royaume-Uni.

institut français

Arcadia Books supports English PEN, the fellowship of writers who work together to
promote literature and its understanding. English PEN upholds writers' freedoms in
Britain and around the world, challenging political and cultural limits on free expression.
To find out more, visit www.englishpen.org, or contact
English PEN, 6–8 Amwell Street, London ECIR IUQ.

Arcadia Books distributors are as follows:

in the UK and elsewhere in Europe:
Turnaround Publishers Services
Unit 3, Olympia Trading Estate
Coburg Road
London N22 6TZ

in the USA and Canada:
Independent Publishers Group
814 N. Franklin Street
Chicago, IL 60610

in Australia:
Tower Books
PO Box 213
Brookvale, NSW 2100

in New Zealand:
Addenda
Box 78224
Grey Lynn
Auckland

in South Africa:
Quartet Sales and Marketing
PO Box 1218
Northcliffe
Johannesburg 2115

Arcadia Books is the *Sunday Times* Small Publisher of the Year

Cast of Characters

MARIA APARECIDA: *Queen of the Square*

GRINGA: *The foreigner*

PIPOCA: *Illiterate, diabetic popcorn seller*

ZÉ and MANUEL: *Teenage lovers, HIV positive*

ORPHAN GABRIELA: *Saucy young prostitute*

SERGIO: *Child vendor of sweets and handkerchiefs*

ANTONIA: *Sergio's mother*

IVONE: *Young, fashion-obsessed convent caretaker*

MAMA LOURDES: *Third-rate clairvoyant*

ONE-EYED TONIO: *Deformed musician*

PIOUS TERESA: *Ageing church mouse*

THE STRAY DOG: *The Square's mascot*

OTAVIO: *Failed writer, alcoholic*

RUBI and SAFIR: *Twin sisters of infinite compassion*

FATHER DENILSON: *Idealistic young priest*

SONIA THE HOOKER: *Ancient tart with a heart*

DR AUGUSTO: *Communist aristocrat*

TURCO: *Dark dashing traveller*

THE TUNER: *Maria Aparecida's son*

NINA from NORDESTE: *An old acquaintance of Maria Aparecida*

SALVADOR

I was born in a small shack, made of any tin and cardboard that happened to be lying around. You may be surprised to hear that I was a happy little girl. Mama was a dressmaker, and I liked to help her, especially for carnival. Sequins, frills and cheap jewellery brightened our wretched lives. Oh, I forgot to tell you: I am Maria Aparecida, a daughter of Iemanja – goddess of the sea – like every girl born in Bahia. You don't need a father when you're a child of the ocean. Look at this bundle of clothes. I've been dragging it around for years; it's my 'home', my sole possession. Mama gave it to me before she died; it was her only legacy. She put all her most beautiful dresses in it for me to sell, and made me swear never to become a dancer. I did promise, to make her feel better, but then the spirit of samba took me. Now, this meagre bundle is all that remains of my past glory and glitzy jewels. Money burned through my hands – my years of debauchery trashed everything. Aparecida the magnificent became the old lady talking to you now. Sometimes, I dreamily imagine myself sitting in one of the brightly coloured *sobrados* that line the Square, leaning on the window and chatting to the birds. But that is too lovely, so to console myself I go and sleep in Father Denilson's church. When the sun goes down I open the little iron gate and take refuge within the faded blue walls. It's not as grand as the basilica, but I like the simplicity – the gold of São José is so dazzling it keeps me awake, and that ill-fated old witch Teresa won't let me in anyway. At the church I have my own little spot, at Nossa Senhora de Aparecida's feet[1]. We share the same name, it brings us closer.

---

1. Patron saint of Brazil.

I am fat, and lazy. Here on our Square overlooking Pelourinho, they've nicknamed me Pipoca because I sell popcorn. It's an easy job, and anyway, to tell the truth I'm no great brain, so... I like beer and sugar, I've got a huge belly, and my diabetes is out of control. I reckon selling popcorn on the Square contributes to public health. Yes, public health! Don't look at me like that, Gringa! For just a few *centavos* I can give kids a treat and tourists a cheap dessert; I can cure heartache... And most importantly, every God-given day I bring delight to thousands of nostrils. Smell the aroma! The sweet, heady perfume of caramel. I can see your eyes sparkling. Come on, have some. You're very cute, Gringa. You find it hard to make out what I'm saying, I can tell. It's always like that to start with. I don't have many teeth left; it's the sugar... But here on the Square everyone gets the gist. The two kids who work for me wouldn't dare take the piss, I can tell you: I explode, just like my namesake. Do I know Maria Aparecida? What kind of stupid question is that? She's the queen of Pelourinho, hand-washing mania and all... She'll drive us nuts with that. But never mind, we look after our Maria.

I'm Zé, and he's Manuel. We're both fifteen. We're queer, and positive. We're homos, fairies, and we love working the tourists who visit the Square. Like you, for example: you've got a nice face, you look like a soft touch. Now what was I saying? Oh yeah, we go up to them with our school uniforms in tatters and cloths over our mouths – look, like this, to stop the illness spreading, you see – and explain that we're sick, and how good it would be if they bought us some grub, some milk or perhaps some soap. Manuel has awful problems with his skin. Sometimes it works, sometimes not – especially when that Aparecida is around. She says we're terrible for business, that we scare away the tourists. It's not true. We never ask for money, we're not beggars. It's just that fortune hasn't exactly smiled on us, and we've done some things we'd rather forget – we had to make ends meet

– but we're too weak now. Oh my, have I shocked you? Calm down, amiga, you can keep your pity. We're hard little buggers. What's your name? Are you Brazilian? You don't seem it, and anyhow, you've got a funny accent. So, Gringa, how about buying us that milk?

No gringo can resist my saucy eyes and angelic face. They saw it coming, at the orphanage: let's call her Gabriela, the nun said, like the archangel. Yeah, right – my name is the only saintly thing about me. To be frank, what the tourists like best are my round buttocks and smooth chocolatey skin. Speaking of which, it's time for work, but I'd better take a good shower first. Nah, tomorrow will do. Of course there's the fountain, but I don't really fancy washing myself in front of the whole Square – you have to pay to see me with my kit off! Oh well, I'll just have to avoid Aparecida. If she saw me like this – can you imagine? She hates it when my hair goes all wild. That old loon doesn't miss a trick. Whenever I wear these too-short shorts, or this skimpy T-shirt, I know I'm good for a slap. She says my boobs are impertinent. Very funny, lady – I need my tits and ass to put food on the table! Nah, I like Aparecida a lot; she's the only one who takes an interest in Orphan Gabriela.

Right, where's that perfumed handkerchief? And my ginger sweeties? It's too dark to see, and I'd like to sleep a bit longer... But Mama will scold me if I'm late. She'll murmur, 'Sergio *querido*, please,' smiling sadly like she has ever since Dad left. In the beginning I thought he'd come back. I used to wait for him every night, but then I realised we were going to be on our own now – Mama, the little ones and me. They're all still hoping he'll come back, Mama especially. I haven't got the heart to tell her the truth. Mama works all the time – washing, ironing, embroidering – but it's not enough. Her pretty, soft hands have become like two rock-hard loaves. I've left school so that my Mama can stay pretty. I help her in any way I can. Mmm, smell this eau de cologne.

Come on, Gringa, buy a perfumed handkerchief! Mama embroidered it. See how lovely it is. Beautiful. And some sweeties. Take at least two packets. One *real* a packet – that's nothing. Good for coughs, sore throats and bad breath. Not that you need it – you smell like a baby, like my youngest sister Taissa. How old am I? Can't you guess? I'm seven. I'm a bit small for my age but... I swear I'm not lying! My name? Sergio. OK, so how about these sweets? We said four *reals*, right? Why are you laughing? Did I say two? I must have got mixed up. Give me four, please, then I can take a *batucada* class. I've always wanted to become a musician. If you give me four, I can get a whole week's worth of lessons. Will you? Thanks. Hey, Gringa, why are there tears in your eyes?

I dream of becoming an actress; a famous actress, like Olympia Wagner. I imagine my name in big letters scrolling across the screen: 'Ivone Santos.' I get shivers just thinking about it. So I take careful note of how the tourists dress, especially the French and the Italians. They're always so elegant, so thin. Apart from that, I listen to the radio. I would have liked to buy a little TV so I could follow the soaps, but the Jesuits won't hear of it. So I just waste away at the top of the stairs of what was once one of the most powerful convents in Brazil. I spend my days taking entry tickets, surrounded by jacarandas and azaleas. People don't even see me. Time has stopped here, and I've stopped with it. I feel as if the mites will eat away at me, just as they do with those ancient bishops' headdresses, of no interest to anyone. Sometimes Aparecida comes to fill her bottles at the tap and we talk. She says God is protecting me here and I'd be dead meat anywhere else. She reckons I'm too beautiful and beauty is misfortune. She knows what she's talking about, that Maria. Who would think that such a dried up old woman was once the pride of Brazil: carnival queen and samba goddess?

Don't say a word. I know who you are and why you're knocking at my door, accursed Gringa. For seventy-six years the gods have been honouring me and using me as their messenger. The whole of Brazil reveres my gifts – even the famous are afraid of me and seek my counsel. Your skin is unlined, but Mama Lourdes can read you: I can read the depths of your soul. Daughter of Iemanja, twenty one *orixas*[2] watch over you. You have come from far away, trying to escape a murky past, but you won't find anything here. Go! Salvador is swarming with malevolent spirits. You don't have to believe me, but be careful: Aparecida is spying on you. Watch out, or she will destroy you.

Everyone on the Square knows me as One-eyed Tonio. I'm always in the same place, next to Cesar's cafe. To tell the truth, an eye isn't the only thing I'm missing – I've also got a wooden leg, and my right hand no longer works. I was born under a sardonic star and soon resigned myself to my condition. I look only on the bright side – who cares about the rest? It's not easy making a living when you're deformed, but God gave me a beautiful deep voice. If I wanted to, I could wrench tears from your lovely eyes – I seduce and survive thanks to my songs. My repertoire is varied but only the sad songs touch me. They make me feel happy and safe, because those who wrote them have suffered, like me. Look, here's Maria Aparecida: she'll want me to sing. It's a pain – she won't let me use my guitar, and what's the point without it? You'll soon learn that. Listen to me, Gringa, I know how to touch your heart. You'll be back tomorrow to listen to One-eyed Tonio.

You're the first, and probably the last, to give me anything today. May God bless you, Gringa. It will soon be thirty years that Pious Teresa has been standing on these stone steps, with only the Bible for company. The Square ignores

---

2. Afro-Brazilian deities.

and despises me. They say I'm sanctimonious and that my faith is nothing but pain. Like Christ, I am crucified – on the lethal, freezing flagstones of the basilica. Morning, noon and night. Neither sun, nor rain nor wind discourages me: I am afraid only of God's wrath. They all sing the praises of the Square – the sturdiness of the trees, the charm of the little houses – but Teresa sees only the misery. Look at these faces: wipe off the make-up, probe the souls and you'll see sadness lurking behind the cheerful masks. Only the Bible can deliver them, but they won't listen to me singing the words of the Lord. On Judgement Day everyone will have to account for themselves; not one shall escape punishment. There shall be no redemption. Only I shall be saved. Aparecida will pay: divine retribution awaits her – the whole basilica isn't big enough to hold her sins. She's asleep in Father Denilson's church now, but a lifetime in hell won't atone for her sins! Pray for her soul, my child. Don't go near her; her mad eyes will contaminate you. Sit down and read this psalm, Gringa; it will protect you.

What mouth-watering smells! And people everywhere! I'm going to have a great time. There's a party tonight, it's a special day. People will be drinking and dancing, they'll be giving off that sweet, strong smell that makes them stagger and drop whatever they're holding in their paws. Straight into my mouth. I'm slobbering already. I'd better watch out, because the other mutts won't miss a trick. There'll be females. I'm off my head with excitement. Let's hope I don't get kicked too many times: if they start wiggling around to music, it's bad news for a stray dog like me. Oh look, here's the old woman with no smell. She's always pouring water over her hands. Honestly, what a nutcase!

I've been hanging around in this bloody cafe for years, sipping bad vodka. Alcohol is the only thing that allows me to tolerate this Square – being drunk makes it seem more lively, less miserable. I came to Bahia in homage to my master and only god, the emperor of Salvador, Jorge Amado. I thought his city might stimulate a little of the talent I naturally lack, but the whores and tramps here have inspired in me nothing but pity and disgust. Just look at that one, the orphan, with her straggly hair: you only have to see her for inspiration to run screaming. But, what an ass! Psst, Gabriela, come here. Get a move on, you silly little whore. I'll have a bit of that – just look at those tits, swaying in time with her hips as she walks. Sit down. What do you want? A kebab! Anything else, m'lady? Get out of here and wash yourself, you stink! The street kids drive me insane. I don't know why I'm still here, poisoning myself with this unspeakable vodka. My talent will go forever unrecognised. The *orixas* never wanted me to succeed – I would have shown up the great Amado. The mad old girl with the red headscarf sometimes says, 'This town has destroyed you, Otavio'. She's the only one who understands that my failure was decreed by fate.

Come over, amiga, and have your photo taken with me. Aren't I pretty in my lace and petticoats? It'll make a lovely memory, full of sunshine and smiles. All I'm asking is a little something towards the upkeep of the outfits. OK? Great. Pipoca, take a photo of us with Gringa. We're going to drown her in goodwill. We sisters, Rubi and Safir, are the pillars of the Square: everyone comes to see us when they're unhappy. We'll cosset you in our caramel arms, tickle you with our frills and flounces until you're as good as new. We do that part for love, we don't take any money. You can ask Maria Aparecida; she loves to come and get a cuddle.

My church is never empty. For the simple reason that the heavy, carved wooden door never closes. The house of God is a refuge for anybody, anytime. The bishop didn't like it, said I was mad, eccentric. But I stood firm. Sure, a few chalices have been stolen, but I don't really mind; they must have needed them. I went to war with the diocese. They claimed I'd taken the side of the wretched and was encouraging their thieving. They can think what they like; I know God doesn't need silver or gold. My congregants have become my friends, my family even. And to think that I was frightened of Salvador, of the *macumba* and *candomblé*[3] here... It's party time when I celebrate Mass inside the sky blue walls of the church. The Square sings its heart out – our voices echo, and bring in the tourists. Sometimes, at dawn, as I'm decorating the altar with flowers, I find Aparecida asleep in a pew. Her face is all serene; only my church brings her peace. My name is Father Denilson, and I'm watching over you.

My body is a sanctuary, it welcomes lost souls. Who else would visit an old whore? Aristos, plebs, hoodlums, perverts – I know them all. I'm not very particular, so long as I get my money. I've not always been that way, but when you get to my age you can't be fussy. I mean, who still wants this old whore Sonia, with her flabby belly and droopy tits? I don't need to worry too much here – the children of the Square are a lovely bunch and they protect me. When trade is good, I go to confession so the Father can absolve my sins. I've grown superstitious over time – being alive after forty years on the job is no accident: it's because the Good Lord wished it so. I've seen so many girls fall to syphilis, alcohol, knives, state custody... Poor things, they weren't good for anything but death. We're very fond of the sweet new Father. He's not full of himself, he's just a person like us. You don't feel guilty with him. Carry on like that and he'll make me feel like a saint. I often use the confessional to get changed; it's private, and keeping my work clothes on outside of hours would be indecent. Once I'm dressed I walk around the Square, greeting and gossiping, hanging out with Rubi and Safir. Over there in the shade of the big jacaranda we have good chats – the tourists, Aparecida and me. Sometimes Sergio joins us. Poor baby, the father ditched his mama,

---

3. Afro-Brazilian rites and rituals, related to voodoo.

him, and the six little ones. Now he's the man of the family, at seven years old. What kind of childhood is that? Anyway, we console each other here, we joke about things. We don't often complain. What good would that do?

Augusto at your service, Gringa. I speak French, like you. I come from one of those powerful families in which it was considered chic to speak the language of Molière. My father, the coffee king, was devoted to me, his only son. But I was bored as a youngster and couldn't think of anything better to do than join the Communist Party. The military dictatorship taught me about torture, cowardice and friendship. I cried like a baby, calling out for my mother. Even now I'm kept awake by the screams of those who didn't talk. Look, my hair's gone prematurely white from fear. So, to forget the pain and control my trembling hands, I became a doctor and fled to Bahia, to the sunlight. I can't handle the dark any more. The children of the Square don't mind having me, and their courage gives me new hope. I don't know why we're such a cheerful lot. It's probably out of discretion – no one wants to hear about unhappiness.

I move around. All I need is my bag and my knives. Music intoxicates me; the rhythm of the drums enchants me like the bodies of lovely mulatto women. I am faithful only to my saint-mistress Bahia. I pay homage to her several times a year, when everything disappears except her musky perfume, her vivid colours and wild waters. Here I am, Salvador. Turco didn't leave you for long.

Gringa – the foreigner. Even here I've become a foreigner. But I was Brazilian just like them, an ordinary woman with simple tastes, part of a smooth and unsurprising story. Then one April morning, I lost my tears. I started roaming, through an endless, constantly moving, hollow universe. My years as a vagabond stripped me of the Carioca accent I was so proud of, that was so much a part of me. A camera slung across my shoulder I travelled the land, scouring it, digging it up, scavenging... I wanted to catch hold of my roots so they would retain me, but my crazy feet kept slipping and sliding. After a while the dreary, depressive photos I took all looked the same. One rainy evening the chapters of my life seemed to start rushing past, with 'THE END' galloping up like a deranged horse. It was time to bring my story to a conclusion, so I came home. Back to Bahia, land of my ancestors.

Time goes by, but people don't change. It's more than fifty years now since I, Nina – a puny little Nordeste girl looking for a better life – landed on the beaches of Bahia. A solicitor employed me to keep house for him and do a bit of cooking. He was a good boss, fair and solitary. He left me a tidy sum when he died, and a room in that pretty pink house near Gringa's. People gossip about what I must have done for a legacy like that, but I don't care – they're just jealous. I spend my days at the window watching the Square and all its children. I've known Maria Aparecida for a long time. We're the same age. People don't believe me, but it's true. You can ask her, although she can't bear my lack of wrinkles so she'd never tell you the truth. Mad Maria, Bahia's brightest flower. She schemed for the downfall of her competitors and was for years the undisputed queen of carnival. She was never cowed by threats or blackmail, and as for scruples... But, dancing and drinking all night, not to mention wickedness, come at a price: you always end up paying. Now that she's withered, her bloom faded, she pretends she's mad. Very convenient. My memory, on the other hand, is a perfectly ordered library. Bitterness has yellowed the pages of the cheapest books, and gnawed them down to the weft, while the beautiful leather-bound ones have stood the test of time – sometimes I even stroke their soft pages. The only man I ever loved was stolen by Aparecida... Thank God there is justice in this world: she has been cursed with a criminal son, the most feared man in Salvador, a bloodthirsty killer. Why else do you think she's always washing her hands?

Strangers won't look at me: they quickly turn their gaze away from the skinny old black woman with the bright red headscarf. My only crime is washing my hands. I'm known for it. I can't help it – it's stronger than me. I'm quite well; I just like washing my hands. My empire has declined over the years. At one time the whole of Salvador worshipped my beauty and paid homage to their carnival queen. They all wanted to touch my light-filled dresses, just to get a bit of my aura. My name is Maria Aparecida, and I still reign over Pelourinho. People think I'm mad, but I'm saner than you.

Drink, Gringa, knock this back in one. No one here under-stands better than me what's happening to you. It's the worst, most cruel punishment. As you know, I am a failed writer and my pen has never produced a single line worth reading. It's Amado's fault. Come on, who do you think you are, drink! The nectar will allow you to forget: it will wipe out your obsessions and dilute your sufferings. Good girl, down the hatch. Come here, Cesar, and give us another – and none of your cheek. Good, isn't it? You'll see, the alco-hol will give you new life, you poor girl. You deserve better than this rotten Square squatted by idiots. You need a man like me: someone who understands and caresses you, like this. That's it, drink some more. You and I are from the same tribe: the tribe of lords and conquerors. You're laugh-ing! Are you drunk? Come here, let me kiss you. OK, on the cheek if you'd rather. That's all you were waiting for, my kisses. Come, Gringa, let's go to my place. You need to be coaxed, like a little girl. Let me kiss you on the mouth. No? Why do you turn your head away? I'm not good enough for you, perhaps? Bitch, you're no better than Orphan Gabriela. Poor little whore. Leading me on with your tear-filled eyes and then coming off all chaste? That's it, insult me. Have you looked at yourself recently? You, an artist? That's right, run off to your barefoot beggars and pathetic whores! Go on, run off and get some sympathy from your wretched tramps – you're no better than them.

God in heaven, Virgin Mary! Augusto the agnostic gives thanks to the Creator – if he does exist, after all. Good work. Gringa has just given the alcoholic writer two massive slaps. At last! What a girl! Who would have said that such fire could explode from such a pale doll? Her stinging slaps rang out over the Square as loud as the *Olodum*[4] drums. You can hear a pin drop in Cesar's cafe. The affront paralysed Otavio. The only response he could think of was to insult Gringa. Not one of the Square's children has gone over to comfort him. He's been spewing out venom for so long, and no one has ever responded to his provocation; we've just let him get away with it, blaming it on his barren imagination. Augusto, undeserving son of the coffee king and disappointed communist, you have found a new heroine.

Bloody hell, Gringa's got character! I'm really glad – I don't like that dirty guy who always stinks of booze. He's nasty, especially with us kids. As soon as we come near Cesar's cafe to sell our sweets and handkerchiefs he clouts us. He even seems to enjoy it. Mama doesn't want me to work near there any more. Sometimes Cesar protects us, but the customer is king and Otavio always pays in the end. It must have hurt, because Gringa hit him really hard. My Gringa. As soon as I see her, I follow her. She always smiles at me and takes me with her on her walks. Sometimes we sit on the steps of Father Denilson's church and talk, like grown-ups. The other day, she treated me to some pastries. I was so happy; it made me feel important. The other kids, even the big ones, were green with envy. And Mama smiled, in her sad way. I must congratulate my Gringa. Maybe she'll let me hold her hand again. It's so soft, like Mama's used to be.

---

4. Well-known Afro band of Bahia.

Neither Manuel nor I know how we sank that low. If only we'd had your courage, Gringa. What a slap! I would like to have given a few of those, but I never knew how, and Manuel was worse than me. From a young age we were told to keep quiet, to accept and obey. When resourcefulness is what counts, you don't argue. You just keep your head down, make yourself invisible. We weren't lucky enough to go to school, Gringa. It was full, and so we took another path. Easy money made us slaves to strangers' bodies. We gave ourselves without even thinking what we were doing. A good samaritan tried to pull us out of that hell, but it was too late. Manuel got sick, and that made me – for the first time – freak out and chuck it all in. We ditched the street, ditched men and glue, and got taken in by the nuns at the community health centre. Our lives consist of laughter and charity: we haven't got much time left, so, like you, Gringa, we prefer to keep quiet about our pain and enjoy these final days.

We've never worked as hard as this: they're all coming to seek solace in our arms. Rubi, overworked, ends up hiding in my skirts. And what about me; who is going to take all this sadness from me? No, don't you worry: I'm packed full of love, and my reserves are still deep. You see, the Good Lord chose not to give me children, so all these people coming to see me are a bit like the son or daughter I never had. I've a soft spot for that Gringa: we've decided to adopt each other. Every time I think about it I feel like doing a jig: Safir, cinnamon mother to porcelain Gringa! Makes you laugh? Me too...

Pipoca is sick as a dog. A tummy bug. Mama made him some gruel, but I don't think he'll like it. He's already scoffed two packets of sweets; I didn't have the heart to stop him. Ivone has put him in one of the convent cells. She says that her Pipoca will be better off there than on a stinking mattress somewhere. Apparently his wife has chucked him out, and so at night he hangs about like a tramp. Poor Pipoca. Dr Augusto said that too much maize was no good, that he would end up popping like his corn. After Maria Aparecida, Pipoca is kind of the boss of the Square, don't you think, Gringa? But for me, the real queen is you. Not counting Mama you're the prettiest. Sergio's honour. And you always smell so good. You won't leave us, will you? You'll stay? Promise?

Orphan Gabriela says that the people of the Square are forgetting their queen, that they've been bewitched by this Gringa. They're in such a state: Turco too well-behaved; One-eyed Tonio beaming senselessly; Rubi and Safir up to their ears; Pipoca in the convent; Augusto so talkative... It's not right. What an ungrateful lot! Forgetting me for such a weedy, pale creature, a vulgar foreigner. No, I won't allow it. Mama Lourdes will help me annihilate this creature who has dared to take my place. The Square hasn't been itself since she arrived. A curse on her!

So, Aparecida, rumour has it that you're finished, washed up, that Aparecida is sinking into oblivion... Ha! Congratulations, O empress of my heart. What have you done to make your subjects abandon you so easily – surely you weren't dethroned by that pale beauty? I never would have thought it possible. Not you, Maria Aparecida, queen of Pelourinho, the only woman I've never been able to bend to my will. How dare they? Don't they fear me any more? Everyone in Salvador dreads and respects my dark eyes. I am known as The Tuner. I use my violin to create unforgettable melodies. This violin was the only thing you ever gave me – you held it out to me one morning, saying that I could survive with it. At the age of eight you can survive anything except being abandoned by your own mother. My instrument is not only a hymn to love but also a fearsome weapon. I can rip off a string, quick as a flash, and slit any bastard's throat. Anyone who looks deep into my eyes slips irremediably into the depths of hell. The murderous string is then put with my other trophies, too many now to count. Tonight, my strings are going to screech.

Gringa, it's me again, Sergio. Mama said I should warn you to be careful. The Square is restless tonight, and we can't find Maria Aparecida. One-eyed Tonio has lost his voice, Zé and Manuel are looking all feverish, Pipoca is fasting, and even Father Denilson has shut himself away in his confessional. People are whispering that it's your fault, the outsider's fault. Sorry, Gringa, but Mama wanted you to know. I know I'm young, Gringa, but I don't believe them. Don't be afraid, I'll protect you. Here, take my hand.

Where on earth is Aparecida? I've been looking for her for hours. Her bundle and bottles are lying by the statue of her saint, which is definitely a bad sign. Ivone says she hasn't been to the fountain today. I can't understand it; this disappearance is very curious. Lord, I'm not happy, not happy at all. I'm even questioning whether to celebrate Mass. Yes, Lord, I am – with all due respect, of course . . .

The spirits are with me, Xango's rage is thundering, I can see his bolts of lightning. People of the Square, the deities are demanding their sacrifices. Evil is on the prowl and death is on its way. I can see it. Hurry, I won't be able to keep it at bay for long. Find Maria Aparecida. That mad old woman is the only one who can save you. Ungrateful people, do not forget your queen, do not trust that Gringa with the too-smooth face. The *orixas* have spoken, O children of the Square. This woman is sowing discord. Get rid of her before the next moon. Before death comes to visit.

It's me, Sonia the pro. This disappearance business is a load of rubbish. I know Queen Aparecida: she's alarming her subjects because she wants us to implore her on bended knees.

One of those old diva tricks. Orphan Gabriela must be in on it, look at her smirking... She's out of control – I'm going to grill her... She owes some respect to her elders after all, cheeky wench.

Jesus, he's gorgeous! He's been driving me wild for years. He's the only one – with all the others I was just passing the time. Oh, he's smiling at me! Look casual, Ivone, be casual, girl. Shit, what with gazing at him all the time I keep forgetting what I'm meant to be doing. I've got to find Aparecida. Maybe she's in the refectory, or perhaps in the garden filling up her bottle. I wish he'd stop looking at me like that – I'll soon be blushing like a debutante. Oh God, he's coming over. Aparecida, Aparecida, where are you? Hello, Aparecida? It's me, Ivone. I should have worn my pink dress today – if only I'd known. Oh, those shoulders, those eyes, how am I supposed to resist? Leave me alone, Turco, not now. Aparecida has disappeared, help me look for her. That's enough, Turco, not here. Aparecida, Aparecida... Turco, no! Aparecida! Come back, save me, save me from this man and his kisses...

As I say the rosary with my red beads, I pray for the Square's sinners, for the salvation of their souls. I wish I could proclaim the words of the Lord loud and clear, but these days my voice is reedy and hoarse. No one listens to me in any case – the Square just pokes fun at 'Saint Teresa' who has given her life to God. Let them laugh, ignorant fools. Only I will be saved. Ivone wants to leave the Square and go south. She would like me to take over from her at the convent and do my preaching in that wicked monastery. But the wealth of the Jesuits disgusts me; I prefer the rough steps of the basilica. I offer my sufferings up to the Lord, as I wait to rejoin Him in His heavenly kingdom. The end is nigh: Aparecida has gone to ground, Father Denilson is no longer master of his flock... Listen to the church bells: they toll the approach of death.

How sweet of you to come and see me, Sonia. People keep coming by, all the time... I'm not dead yet, you know. Pipoca may be fat, but he's indestructible; and Ivone is looking after me like a daughter. So much kindness. I come over all funny just thinking about it; I'm not used to it. The only bad things are the smell of mothballs and these saints looking down on me with their sorrowful eyes. When I go for a piss at night I get such a shock when I come across them in these long, lifeless corridors. The convent is beautiful – that goes without saying – with its parquet floors, jacaranda-wood furniture and richly decorated ceilings. But I wouldn't live here for the world, no, I wouldn't – it's too big and too refined. All this gilding and these silently suffering saints make me nervous; I can't wait to get back to the Square and my popcorn! What about you, old girl? How's trade? Someone told me that Gringa slapped Otavio. Bravo! Though she'd better watch out: he's a fearsome enemy to have. But don't you worry, we're all friends at the Square and we'll protect her. If only our loony lady would do us a favour and come back...

Can I have a word, Gringa? Are you in a rush? It'll only take a minute, please. Follow me, we can go to the garden – it's the only happy place in this whole convent. I take my breaks here. Sometimes I share my lunch with the birds. Yes, it's me, Ivone. Gorgeous, isn't it? I love these ancient trees with their knotty roots and green leaves, luminous with sap. But I haven't brought you here to admire nature. It's just, you're educated, you come from far away... I need your advice. I want to go away, to leave this convent. I can't stand this life any longer. What would I like to do? Be an actress. Over in São Paulo. D'you think I stand a chance? In Rio or São Paulo? No, I'm not scared. The Square? Well, I've got to leave one day. Turco? I'll soon get bored with him. The only thing keeping me here is my Pipoca. I wanted to ask you – will you look after him? Just pop by and see him once in a while? Yes? You promise? Thanks, Gringa – I knew you'd

17

help me. You're a lovely girl, Gringa. I like you a lot, even if you are a bit quiet.

I can't stop thinking about Ivone: her body, her green, green eyes... But what's the point? She'll soon be off to São Paulo, to be an actress. Honestly! But why not? She'll drive them all wild with that face. Perhaps she'll make me famous, too... Have to wait and see... And you, Gringa? Will you let me taste your translucent skin? Sweet mysterious stranger, you won't be able to resist me. Turco's honour.

How strange... I can hear music. It's a violin, I think. Who could it be, playing under my window on this moonless night? It's too dark for me to seek you out, sad song. Another time, perhaps. Usually, the lanes of Pelourinho help soothe my insomnia. Once the Square is sleeping I leave my room and take a walk around the churches. When I raise my head I see the stars smiling at me. The sky here is so clear. Sometimes I come across Orphan Gabriela working, or Pipoca wandering around morosely – poor lost soul. We greet each other silently and continue on our way. At night, people's secrets are their own. I return exhausted after these long solitary walks and fall into a dreamless sleep. I won't manage that tonight – I'm too haunted by images of the past, futile memories that my brain won't release.

Violins are a forewarning of tragedy on this Square. But who dares talk about it? The only one to brave taboos here is Otavio; the alcohol gives him courage. He'll be hushed one of these days. Gringa is cocooning herself in silence, although she sometimes hums a refrain during her night-time wanderings, a heart-rending lullaby from another world. My voice sounds terrible since Aparecida disappeared, and I daren't touch my guitar; the baleful, tuneless notes it produces upset me too much.

Zé is coughing constantly. Lying snuggled up we listen to

our hearts beating, and they sound so tired. We'd better beg for some cough syrup tomorrow; just for the short term. Or sugared water if we can't get syrup. Zé, listen a minute. Jesus! I know that sound... Stop coughing! D'you hear what's going on, Zé? It's The Tuner; no one else plays like that. Let go of me, I want to see. Don't worry, it's safe. And anyway, I'm already half-dead... He's sitting under the porch, Zé, with his violin. Gringa's light has just come on. Oh God, no! We can't let this happen. Calm down, Zé, I've got to go and tell Gabriela – she's hustling near by, and she knows where mad Maria is. Nothing will happen to me, I promise. That's enough, Zé. If it's already too late, it'll be on your conscience. Right, I'm off. Don't worry, I will be back.

Not many clients tonight. Nothing but winos! I'm going home, I'm knackered – a little holiday won't do me any harm. Who's that over there? Looks like Turco, but what the hell is he doing here? It's not like him to wander around like that. He's not come to see me, that's for sure – chicks would pay him for sex! Ivone reckons he's the fuck of the century. She's got it bad, poor thing; I've never seen her like this. I'm going to follow him, for Ivone's sake. Where the hell is he going? Oh wow, a violin. But a violin... can only mean one thing! Jesus Christ, get out of here, Gaby, before the blood starts flowing.

What's that music? Oh great, now I'm hallucinating. I've never been a jumpy guy, you've got Pipoca's word on that. But just now I'm in pretty bad shape. I haven't had a single beer since Ivone put me in this blessed convent. A nice cold beer... Bloody hell, I'd give anything for a pale, icy ale. I'll never get back to sleep now. I've got to get out of this tomb. Sonia told me earlier that a whole load of priests are buried under the chapel flagstones. How am I supposed to get better here?

I may have acted the tough guy in front of Zé, but actually

I'm freaking out. I don't know what got into me; this is suicidal! There's no sign of Gabriela anywhere; this whole business is going to end up in the morgue, I can feel it. Oh look, there's Turco. Where's he going? Ave Maria, no, no, no. Such a good-looking boy. I can't let him get his throat cut like this... Gringa, at a pinch, but not him. Zé would kill me. I know he's got a soft spot for him...

Come to me, pale beauty. Give me your secret, white shadow. Open yourself to me. I will drive you crazy with my violin, O cursed Gringa envied by the mother-queen. Show yourself! Let me steal a little of your power. Listen to my violin and speak.

I feel the notes sweeping over me, round and sensual. They caress me, brush against me with husky breath. My skin is throbbing and craving more. The melody is getting bolder, taking possession of the room, insinuating itself into the very depths of my being. The music gathers speed, builds gently in me, pulls back and then rallies hard to penetrate me. And suddenly that April morning disappears at last, carried away by this bewitching violin.

Pelourinho is deserted. The night is dark and silent, but I can see shadows: I'm being followed. Not for long. Turco will teach you a lesson, you crook – the knife bristling against my thigh is yearning to plunge into your flesh. I've no time to lose: Ivone is waiting for me. I can hear footsteps behind, and a violin in the distance.

Aparecida has gone a bit far this time. I haven't celebrated Mass for two days, and the congregation is grumbling. My vacant church is bored, the organ is gathering dust, and even the candles seem sad; they aren't giving off their usual glow. As for the bishop, he is delighted... Perhaps a little stroll will calm me down.

I can smell tragedy. It's me, the stray dog. I know this neighbourhood better than you, and something's been wrong for a while now. All the other mutts have scattered, driven away by the sour stink of fear. And now this music, like a scream. The alleys are swarming with people tonight. But instead of noticing each other they are all just moving blindly towards the same point, following these shrill notes that prefigure death.

Aparecida, Aparecida! Stop that, let go, it hurts. Listen to Orphan Gabriela. Aparecida, listen to me. It's important, I beg you, it's very serious. Don't look at me like that – I haven't betrayed you. You know very well you're like a mother to me. Aparecida, it's your son. Yes, your son, the one whose name must never be spoken. He's playing under Gringa's window. Do you know what that means? Stop washing your hands and run. Hurry up, you old loon! You're the only one who can change what is about to happen...

Miserable slums... Ancient hovels that should be demolished. Colourful, you say! These shacks all look the same... Disgusting... Only idiotic tourists think this area is 'charming'... What bullshit... I mean look at these paving stones, awful... They make me trip... Oops... I don't want to dirty my white suit, it looks so good on me... I would have had one for the road, but I can't bear that Cesar looking down on me, or this sordid Square. Who exactly do these tramps think they are? WHO, HUH? My pain is much worse than theirs. Isn't that the little whore... Hey... Come here, you bitch. You don't want me, handsome Otavio, the lady's man? Hey... Come over, sweet negress... I'll show you what Otavio's made of. That's it, run away, you'll be better off... Unbelievable! Some idiot playing the violin in the middle of the night. Who could it be?

I can feel your heart racing, Gringa. Open yourself, tell The

Tuner. Give yourself over to my violin. Feel this melody; it's caressing you... Let it guide you to me. What's that noise? Wait here, Gringa, don't go.

What, this awful musician is at Gringa's? Well, well, well, it seems our haunted beauty has a suitor. Hey you, Mr Violin, that's enough of your wailing. I can't see your face, you idiot... Come closer so I can see your mug... Come closer if you're a man. Hark if it isn't Aparecida's bastard! The fearsome Mama's boy who strikes terror into our beggars' hearts! Ha, ha. Trying to pick up the new queen, are you? Your mother is finished, kid. And anyway, she was never anything but a whore, like all the others... Huh, bastard? Know what I'm talking about, huh?

Is that you, Pipoca? What are you doing here? Be reasonable, Dr Augusto said you were to stay in bed for two more days. Do stop with all that 'Father' business, please. My name is Denilson and I'm first and foremost your friend. So anyway, what are you doing here on this moonless night? You got depressed in the convent? Well, I can understand that. Yes, the Square feels strange to me tonight, too. The stray dog has been hanging around under my feet for a while now, and see how oddly he's looking at us: as if he is afraid. Any news of Aparecida? Nothing, amigo, not even a whisper...

Play, oh play some more, I beg you. I don't know who you are, dark shadow, but do keep playing, please; you're the only one who understands. I can hear footsteps and muffled cries. Play, play some more, silence all those voices. Why this sudden quiet? What's going on?

Did my knife scare you? You must be crazy, Manuel, following me in the dead of night! You're shaking... Calm down and come for a drink; you need one... What's going on, kid? Tell me, for God's sake. I can't understand what you're saying. Who? Calm down, Manuel, you're quite safe with me, Turco. I'll protect you. The Tuner? Gringa? Serenading under her window? A mortal melody? Get out of here quick, Manuel, and wait for me at the Square.

Put away your knife, Turco. Get rid of Manuel; it wouldn't be right for him to see this ugly sight, this pool of red blood on a white suit. Otavio died as pitifully as he lived. By the hands of my creation, my flesh and blood, my shame. My son. He is haunting me, right here on the Square. The son seeking revenge on his negligent mother, carnival queen pitted against violin emperor. Come and see, Turco, under Gringa's window. Come and see my creation.

The pack is converging. For the first time ever the mother is looking for me. Come, then, you'll find me tonight. Your pitiless eyes will curse me but I will confront you. I am no longer the little boy who begged for a glance, a single gesture, even a sharp word. All my life I've waited for you, willing to forgive, to forget the nonchalance that made you so beautiful. The barrier of madness has long allowed you to ignore my crimes, but tonight you can no longer escape. The Square is waiting for you... But first, dear queen, your prince will play for you – one last time – the gypsy tune you used to love so much. The tune you no longer dare listen to: the one my father sang to you before he hanged himself. Weep, O mother, and curse your son. I am safe at Gringa's; you cannot hurt me. My true queen is sleeping like an angel, unaware that the devil and his violin are watching over her.

The smell of fresh blood makes its way into dreams. The children of the Square are waking up, intoxicated by its wild fragrance. They are flying the flag of hate. No one is weeping for Otavio's pitiful demise. I watch from my window for the arrival of Aparecida, the woman I have hated for so many years. That harpy wrecked my life. She couldn't bear our happiness, and so she had to destroy it. I am not beautiful; I've never had her style. To my man, her voice was honey and her eyes melting pools. Bewitched, he left me one carnival night. But Aparecida is an insatiable vampire and soon she needed new victims, fresh blood. Abandoned, my man hanged himself one Ash Wednesday. He didn't know that he had breathed life into the body of his queen, didn't know that a new victim would be born that Christmas. Nina from Nordeste has no mercy; the time of reckoning has come. Now that she is being forced to face her nightmares, Queen Aparecida's reign will soon collapse.

Manuel is holding tight to me, his hand melting into mine. How moving this hunger for life, this bravery – and I used to think he was soft. Zé already knows what's going on and when he sees us, he gives us a huge hug, delighted that we're still in the land of the living. They exchange glances and I feel their love, and envy them. If only Ivone could teach me.

I'm scared. I should have listened to Mama for once and stayed quietly at home. But I couldn't just sit there waiting for disaster – I love Gringa too much. Who else would hold my hand and treat me to pastries? Who else would stroke my hair for hours? I've got to save her. From up here on the roof I can just make out The Tuner, and Gringa sleeping next to him. My heart is beating so hard it hurts my ears. And I've got this awful urge... My eyes are stinging, but I mustn't cry. I hate being little. I want to be like Turco. I've never been one for prayers, but right now I'd give all the sweets and coins in the world to know one.

My fingers quiver, they drum and tease. Travelling all over you, pinching you, they lose themselves in your amber surface. I am fascinated by your curves. I know them so well from the lonely nights playing and exploring with my bow. Look, cursed violin, Gringa is waking. Her eyes gaze at me without fear, and now the innocent girl sits up and kisses me gently on the forehead: a chaste gift in return for these peaceful hours. Her serene face is radiant with goodness, and she's smiling at me. Death can wait. Take this violin, Gringa, and give it to Maria Aparecida, who has never looked at me with the sweetness I see in your eyes. No, I won't play for you any more. One-eyed Tonio will have to take my place. Goodbye, Bahia.

Look at them come. I can see them all flocking towards the Square. They wave at me here between my blue shutters. The sun will be attending, too – it is gradually joining the others. Maria Aparecida is waiting regally on the church steps. Her body is held to attention, the truth making it rigid. The end is nigh. She waits, resigned, for her son. But Nina knows he will deliver the ultimate insult, he won't come. Sergio is dozing next to me. He slipped in under the tiles, looking for a cuddle. It seems The Tuner fled, transformed, over the rooftops.

All my children are here. Safir whimpering for her porcelain Gringa while Rubi fusses over her; Pipoca sipping a beer under the disapproving eye of the doctor; Father Denilson making his church ready for a last homage to Otavio – he says we must forgive; Ivone plaiting Antonia's hair with Turco keeping watch near by; Dr Augusto sweating even though the sun has not yet risen; One-eyed Tonio whistling; Mama Lourdes and Pious Teresa predicting the worst; Orphan Gabriela munching something as she rests her head on Sonia the pro's shoulder. The dog slips into the church looking for Father Denilson. Sergio waits next to Nina, who is staring at me with her usual hatred. Maria Aparecida, queen of Pelourinho, did not abandon you for long.

I will find Maria Aparecida, I will keep my promise. Violin in hand I scour alleys, public gardens and churches. The musician vanished. I'll have to forget the suffering in his sad eyes, the beauty of his hands, his silences. But his notes accompany me, they will be with me forever. My fingers grip the strings of his violin, shaky to start with but soon recovering their agility – and for the very first time they play the lullaby from that April morning of a whole other life.

Whose clear voice is that, singing? The whole Square is holding its breath, all its children have frozen. Gringa approaches, looking determined. Her eyes widen in astonishment at seeing everyone assembled like this, but she quickly gets hold of herself when she sees Aparecida standing stiff as a statue, eyeing her with icy scorn. Gringa walks forward with great resolve and holds out the violin to her, a cursed offering. Aparecida shrinks back, transfixed. She sags and totters, then rallies fast. She descends the church steps, knocks over her bottles, and disappears.

RIO DE JANEIRO

Mama Lourdes is leaning against her door, smoking a cigar. Sergio hurries past, pretending not to see her. But the voo-doo priestess calls out to him in that gravelly voice he hates. Her eyes are piercing; he can feel them scouring and upsetting him. Best not to turn around. The Square isn't much further.

He is enveloped in curls of smoke. It's getting into his nose and throat, and the smell is making him dizzy. His vision goes all hazy as he is overwhelmed by the cold tobacco mixed with a sickly sweet smell of musk on withered skin, a foreshadower of death and decomposition. Sergio comes to a standstill, trying not to vomit. A bangle-laden hand swoops down on to his shoulder, clasping and bruising him. A hand of iron, greedy and implacable. Mama Lourdes looks down at him with a sardonic smile. Sergio longs to scratch her, or launch a giant gob of spit right at her face. He isn't intimi-dated by this witch, isn't scared of her like all the cowards on the Square. He's never believed in her tourist *macumba* – her magic has done nothing but rob him of his savings. She disgusts him. Sergio struggles, unable to bear her touch a moment longer. 'Don't run like that. It's done. You can't change a thing, and nor can Gringa. No one can help you, Sergio. Forget her and go.'

Sergio throws himself on Mama Lourdes in a rage, in the grip of a monstrous fear. He bites her arm, and she lets him go. He runs off, leaving her curses behind him. Mama Lourdes is a liar: his Gringa will speak to his mother, his Gringa will make her stay.

At last he arrives at the Square. It has never looked so beautiful. Gringa is sitting on the church steps chatting to Pipoca. Sergio dodges behind Cesar's cafe to wipe his face with the back of his hand and smooth his ruffled hair, and then takes a step towards her. A mysterious power stops him going any further. He feels dizzy and grabs hold of a chair. Gringa is only a few metres away, but she is looking at him helplessly; she can't do anything either. He shuts his eyes but quickly opens them again. This is the last time; he wants to engrave her face on to his memory. Gringa stands up and holds out her arms, calling to him. Sergio turns and flees in the opposite direction, the gravelly voice gaining ground, coming to get him, chanting incomprehensible litanies. Enough to drive him insane.

A new life, we needed a new life. That was Mama's favourite phrase; she used to say it all the time. I must have been looking at her funny, because she got down on her knees, took my face in her reddened hands and said, 'Sergio *querido*, you've got to understand: sweets are all very well, but you deserve more than that. When you grow up, you're going to be a doctor.' My heart beat wildly. Doc-tor. Doc-tor. The word suffocated me, I felt choked. Mama was asking the impossible, and anyway, I wanted to be a rapper like my hero MV Bill. She was forgetting where we came from: no one knew any doctors round our way. Well, apart from Dr Augusto at the Square. But the doctors we knew best were on the soaps. Oh, we knew the soaps all right – they were part of the family and they were giving Mama ideas above her station. Whenever lovers were reunited she would hide her tears, thinking of Dad. If he hadn't left, she would still have pretty hands and I wouldn't have left school. All this sadness sometimes made me feel like crying. But I couldn't, now that I was the man of the house. I promised her whatever she wanted, kissing her fingers ruined by washing and icy water. I couldn't really understand why she wanted to go to Rio to look for work. Everyone knew there wasn't any work in Rio. And even if there was, you couldn't find anywhere to live, especially with seven kids. But Mama insisted that she wanted to get away from Bahia. I was eight years old, and whenever Rio came on the TV – the attacks on buses, the stray bullets and war-torn favelas – I got so scared I couldn't sleep. If we were there, how could I protect everybody? How would I manage so far away from my Gringa? I visited Nossa Senhora de Aparecida in Father Denilson's church, but it didn't do any good, so I went to see Mama

Lourdes. In any case, neither saints nor *candomblé* stood a chance against Mama. Rio would change our lives.

When we got off the bus it was raining. One of those fierce, heavy summer rainstorms. The mountains seemed threatening, as if they were blocking our way. Between us and the city centre was a whole series of obstacles – bridges, tunnels, motorways, traffic jams. The little ones were soaked and crying, so we stopped well short of the sea and the beaches. Mama was clutching her suitcases as though she had packed all her dignity and last hopes inside them. I could see that she was regretting leaving the Square. In front of us were creepy-looking hills covered with shacks. I felt lost just looking at them. The shacks were like leeches, stuck all over the mountains, devouring them. I couldn't see how it all stayed standing – it seemed to me that the rain and the wind were about to wash it all away. How would we manage to live in this gigantic rat warren? Buses kept roaring past on their way to Copacabana, Lagoa, Botafogo, Jardim Botânico, and I wanted to leap on to the next one and disappear. It was no longer raining, and all of a sudden night fell. The damp seeped into our bones as a few starving buzzards circled the air above us. And then the shacks disappeared in the dark, and the hills lit up, and you couldn't tell the difference between the starry sky and the thousands of little lights. It was magical. We felt much better, and so we walked towards the closest favela, Widow's Hill.

The kids were laughing, and Mama's pretty smile was back; she was singing. I felt more of a man than ever, copying MV Bill and his totally cool swagger. We walked into what seemed to be the main street. It was six o'clock. Workers arriving home, buses unloading their cargo of uniformed schoolkids, old people out strolling arthritic limbs on the uneven pavements. Women calling to each other from window to window, husbands playing cards or dominos, young people drinking beer on the steps and listening to the radio.

There were steps everywhere; so many I couldn't count them all. And enormous queues for the little diners where TVs were playing. It smelled great – fresh *pastelzinhos* and well-cooked *churrasco*. Mama and I looked at each other. It felt good here. We decided to stay and treat ourselves to a proper meal in a 'per kilo' restaurant. We had only just finished when some bikers arrived. They had enormous guns and were shouting orders all over the place. I was frozen to my chair and couldn't understand a word of what they were saying. We were kicked out of the restaurant – the guy had to close. The dealers were waiting for a big delivery. The roads emptied in a flash, and we couldn't understand where everyone had gone. We found ourselves in the middle of the main drag with all our stuff. There was no one around, just shops with their metal shutters down. Three bikers came over and cornered us. They were showing off and taking the piss out of our battered suitcases and the dirty clothes we'd been travelling in. A boy not much older than me jumped off his motorbike and put a gun to my youngest brother Edmilson's head. I leapt on him, exactly what he was waiting for. Mama tried to intervene but one of the guys got her by the hair and dragged her off into a corner. I was screaming and those bastards were laughing at me. Then a shot went off. I can't remember anything after that. Except for two letters tattooed on one of the gunmen's arms. CV. *Commando Vermelho*.

After that it was all over. Fucked. Finished. I woke up in some sleazy room. It stank. There must have been twenty of us in there. I looked around for Mama and the kids, but I couldn't see anyone I knew. I don't know why, but I started thinking about the Square. I wanted to see Gringa and everyone again. I tried to get up to find them, but I collapsed on the mattress. It was a disgusting, stained mattress that stank of piss. A fat black woman came over and put her hand on my forehead. She told me to keep quiet, suddenly looking very strict – you wouldn't mess with her. When she saw I was about to wail she softened and told me I was in a clandestine hospital and that she saw cases like mine every day. I kept telling her that I had to see my mother, and my brothers and sisters, but she didn't want to know. I wasn't to move, boss's orders. Boss? What boss? There was a silence then, and everyone looked at me like I was crazy. Among the graffiti and images of the Virgin Mary on the walls were those same letters, CV. I started yelling, and the fat black lady – Eunice, her name was – gave me a slap and told me to shut it. She offered me a sip of coconut milk and went off grumbling that she had other people to look after. On the next mattress was another boy, a black kid like me. He didn't look too great either. He told me proudly that he had been shot twice in the legs but had done his job and got the dead man's gun. A .50 calibre rifle, a real gem. I made out that that was cool, even though I knew nothing about weapons apart from the AK-47s in MV Bill's videos. He asked if I had killed yet, but then said no, I was still a bit young. He gave me two years until my first cartridge. I did some sums: he was offering me a police record for my tenth birthday. My mind was whirling, and I felt a terrible urge to throw up. But I didn't want to seem like a wimp, so I thought of Gringa and that helped a bit. Eunice was watching me out of the corner of her eye and told my neighbour to give it a rest. He laughed and shut up straight away. I went back to sleep, and when I woke Mama was there, like a ghost. The kids were there as well, but two were missing. I asked where they were but nobody replied. It was then that I understood the shots.

There used to be eight of us, but now there were only six – or five in a way because Mama didn't really count any more. Eunice took us in and told me not to worry about the rent. She offered me a job at the hospital as rent for all of us. The boss – 'The Philosopher' – had told her to. They called him that because he had his own ideas: stuff about revolution. Thanks to him, the community had improved. He had built two new schools, a crèche and an amazing sewerage system.

People in the favela liked him. Sure, his business was dope, but no one had ever seen him smoke or snort, or even drink. He was known to read a lot, and you don't often get educated gang leaders, so the whole favela was proud of our Philosopher. He had heard about Edmilson and Adriana, and he wasn't pleased. Killing and thieving within Widow's Hill was not OK. It attracted the police and gave the place a bad reputation. The three bikers were tried and then punished with a bullet in the head. The Philosopher did it himself – from time to time he liked to set an example. I wanted to thank him, but he didn't stay long in any one place so I couldn't. But he heard, saw and knew everything, so he got the message. Renato, Percival, Luciana and Taissa were at school, and I helped out at the secret hospital. In the beginning it was like hell. I wasn't used to all the blood, or the pressure. People banging on the door, panic, guys arriving in a total state, girls for abortions, junkies stealing medication... Little by little I got to know people's jobs from their injuries. Carpenters, bricklayers, mechanics – something always gave it away. Or the bullets told you. The further up the guy was in the hierarchy, the bigger the weapon. Most of the time I worked with my headphones on and MV Bill blasting. He and the letters from Gringa that Eunice read out to me were the only things that got me through. MV Bill came from the City of God, one of the roughest favelas, and still lived there even though he was a star. He wasn't scared of anyone – not dealers or cops, and definitely not politicians. To start with Eunice made a fuss; she didn't think much of me rapping while I worked, but in the end she put up with it. She would say that for once a black from the favelas had made it – not as a crook – and that we should follow his example. I liked Eunice. She looked after Mama and took her along to church to cheer her up. Some kind of evangelical thing where a preacher in a slick suit boosted their spirits. One thing I couldn't understand was why he took ten per cent of their wages. Mama didn't have any wages so she gave her wedding ring. I thought that was a good sign: she must have forgotten Dad. I didn't worry, because she went with Eunice. What a mistake.

To tell the truth, I didn't realise what was going on because I didn't have time. Eunice and I left for the hospital at seven. Once we got there, time flew. We cleaned up all the mess from the night – lookouts, managers, frontliners, errand boys and battered women. All kinds of low life. Eunice and a retired nurse sewed, cut, tidied and consoled. I cleaned, sponged, helped. After a bit they wanted to put me in charge of telling people their relatives had died, but I wouldn't. I withdrew to the dispensary in protest. It became my zone, I loved it there. It seemed a long time ago that I was quietly selling sweets on the Square. Caramels, lollipops and chocolate had been replaced by meds. When someone was really in pain I would make them a special cocktail. I chose the brightest coloured pills – they were bound to work great. OK, so we went through loads of meds, but I got some mates to source me more. Whenever they went to do a bank in town, I asked them to pass by the pharmacy on their way. As long as the cops weren't right on their tail they always came back with something. They seemed to enjoy it. They were nicking for the community – more fun than robbing tourists. The 'pharmacy gang' was even in the papers. They thought we were stealing meds to copy them and make fakes with flour – and you know what: that wasn't such a bad idea. The only problem with my mates was that they usually had to work very fast, so they took whatever they could lay their hands on. They brought me some really useless stuff. I had tanning lotion, anti-wrinkle cream and nicotine patches coming out of my ears. About every other time I got alcohol, aspirin and coloured pills. I was clear about what I needed: pink, blue and yellow ones. I always found them the most effective.

At exactly midday I would leave everything and rush off by motorbike-taxi to pick up the kids from school. Mama didn't go because she wasn't strong enough to climb all those steps. I was never once late – I made sure not to be. About twenty of us guys would be there waiting for kids – most of them dads, older, but they knew I was head of the family, so no one treated me any different. We used to wait on the pavement discussing the teachers, and how the kids were getting on, boasting, comparing results and often punishments too. The mothers worked in the city, down in the valley. In their jobs as servants, shop assistants, hairdressers and checkout girls they hardly had time to grab a bite, never mind go up to collect the kids at lunchtime. So it was down to us guys to look after the little ones. We went to get them, carried their satchels, brought them home to eat and do their homework. It was a bit tricky for me, with four satchels and all their little hands clinging to my shorts. I didn't want anyone to feel left out, so I created a system. The boys held my hands on Mondays, the girls on Tuesdays, and so on until Friday. That way everyone was happy. We all ate lunch together – with Mama and Eunice – and then I took them to the 'Tomorrow's Smile' club, where they learned painting and music and stuff like that. I never let them play in the street by themselves – it was too dangerous. Then one of my mates told me that a frontliner had taken on my brother Renato to keep watch over the streets. He was so proud of himself and prayed for a police car to enter his zone, so he could alert the hill by flying his skull and crossbones kite and become a hero overnight. Moron. When I heard that, he got the biggest thrashing of his life. Eunice and Mama had to tear us apart. He wanted to kill me for showing him up in front of his friends. The girls didn't give me much bother, except that I always had to bring them presents: what did I know about girls' stuff? I had to rack my brains every week to think of what to get them. But it was always worth it when I saw how happy they were. One day I found something really cool. Like the salesman said, it was a rarity, a toy fit for princesses. We bargained hard and I managed to get a good deal. They were all speechless when I brought it home.

Eunice looked pretty stern, but Mama and the others were shrieking with delight. I reckoned it would give me a bit of peace. I couldn't have been more wrong.

The hospital didn't pay much, but I was the king of blag. The kids' school fees were paid for by the boss. He even wanted to give me a hi-fi so I could listen to MV Bill at home. The Philosopher was a big MV Bill fan, too; I think they even knew each other. But Eunice decided there was no room in our little house and so it could wait. I didn't believe her, and I was going to protest, but then I just shut up. The thing is, Eunice was trying to protect me, to stop me from becoming part of the system. First you get the hi-fi, then you want cable TV, new trainers... Eunice couldn't understand why kids round our way needed Nikes. But then Eunice was clueless about fashion. Yes, even kids round our way had to have Nikes, which meant that when the traffickers tempted us with three hundred *reals* a week, it wasn't easy to say no. You could make twice as much cash in a week as your parents made in a month. We reckoned we looked like the kids at the American school down in the valley, which cost twenty thousand dollars a year. You know, classy. Eunice was always saying that everyone had their place, and that's where they belonged. That really pissed me off. If I was supposed to stay in my place, then why did she want me to become a doctor? If you ask me, Eunice didn't make sense sometimes. Sure, I'd have liked the three hundred *reals* a week, but I didn't really want to hold up a bank or anything like that. I was eight years old. That was the best age for dealing and killing because when you came of age the judge wiped your record clean. It was a top law that worked for everyone: kids got to cut their teeth and make some cash, the big guys didn't run any risks, and if the kids fell like flies settling their own scores – well, that just made the cops' job easier. Your life expectancy dropped like a stone once you got into the system. If you were still alive at twenty-five, you were a boss. Eunice knew all this, and then Mama got her

started on the doctor business. Between them, they'd probably get their way. Like I was saying, the hospital didn't pay
me much, so when I had time I would go to people's houses
and treat them there; if they couldn't move, or if going to
hospital was too risky for them. That's how I met my mates
Sardine and Chiclete. Mostly I got paid in cash, especially by
the crims. But the others would sometimes barter, with
cloth, meat, gas bottles, rice… Anything really. People
started calling me Doc. That really put the shits up me,
because I couldn't cure everyone. I was scared that some
idiot would think it was my fault and seek revenge. Once,
someone held his Colt 38 to my head saying, 'Save my buddy
or you'll be joining him.' I got the shakes and couldn't do
my stitches. Sweat was dripping in my eyes. Luckily it wasn't
a deep wound and I managed, and the guy was totally
impressed. He gave me a big wad of notes and slapped me
on the shoulder like a man. He told me that if I needed any
help I could ask for Purgatory. How's that for a name! I did
some research and found out that the guy came from Cave
Hill and was a frontliner for Commando Vermelho. He was
a trigger-happy lunatic, so I was glad he liked me. By now
people were recognising me in the street and sometimes even
asking me in for a *feijoada*.[5] The superstitious ones would
touch my head; they reckoned it brought them luck. In spite
of all this, I still hadn't got my head round Adriana's and
Edmilson's deaths. But, thank God, there was a great vibe at
home since that infamous present: Pirate, the parrot.

The salesman had sweet-talked me, saying that the parrot
spoke really well and was an exceptional bird, even if he only
had one eye. He called him Bandeira because his colours
matched our flag – yellow and green feathers and a blue
crest. All that was missing was 'Ordem e Progreso' branded
on his head. The bird certainly had the gift of the gab. He
hadn't shut up since I'd walked into the shop. What I liked

---

5. Pork and bean stew traditionally eaten on Sunday afternoons.

best was his eye patch, just like Captain Hook's in *Peter Pan*. All he needed was a three-cornered hat – which is how he went from Bandeira to Pirate. I hesitated for quite a while before taking him because I knew Eunice wouldn't be too happy. Then he started mimicking the salesman's endless banter, which really cracked me up. I could just see the kids' faces, them clapping their hands and all that stuff. OK, so as soon as I saw him I did imagine teaching him MV Bill songs, but I swear I bought him for the kids. The salesman put him in a nice big cage. I wondered where we would put it, because there wasn't much space at home. Mostly though, I worried about the heat, which was our biggest problem – the cement held it in, and we still didn't have a fan. I soon realised that although we'd figure out the space and heat issues, the rest wasn't going to be easy. By the rest, I mean Eunice. In two hours Pirate had created the most unbelievable mess in the house – the guy had forgotten to tell me that this parrot was a real pig. Which may be why he and Eunice hated each other from the word go. The kids were trying to pull out his feathers and managed to let him out of his cage. Once he was out, he started flying round the house knocking everything over, which was pretty bad news since seven of us lived in two tiny rooms. Mama was screaming because he'd got hold of her hair, the girls were laughing their heads off, Renato was trying to pin him with a knife and Percival was hiding under the kitchen table. Meanwhile I was getting bawled out in the next-door neighbour's front yard. The whole street was leaning out of their windows to see where the yelling was coming from; they thought we'd had an accident. Eunice was hollering enough to make herself hoarse, she was so mad. The real reason she was so wound up was because Pirate had been yelling 'Fatty!' for the last ten minutes, and everyone was chuckling. Eunice didn't think it was funny at all. She swore she'd cook the parrot for Sunday lunch. Then I remembered the salesman telling me that if I had any problems, I should give him some birdseed and that would keep him busy. I left Eunice mouthing off to the neighbour and ran off to get the seed. Renato had already swallowed half the packet. He thought they were very tasty and didn't want to give them to Pirate, but Pirate had seen his seeds and was flying around above our heads not looking too pleased. The ceiling was so low that his wings bashed against the light bulb and shattered it, so now we were in pitch-blackness. It was silent for a moment and then someone lit a match. A man in uniform. A policeman from the BOPE, the elite squad, had come for a routine search. We all stopped laughing. Even Pirate.

The guy was alone, which was a good sign. At least it wasn't a death squad. They never came alone, and they hid their faces, although people knew they were mostly military police. Eunice had come up with a torch pretty sharpish, and politely asked the guy if he could help her to replace the light bulb. He hesitated a moment, taken aback by her friendly tone – it must have been unusual for him. Eunice always did know how to play things. Meanwhile I was freaking out about Pirate. He was contraband, so if the cop discovered him we'd end up at the police station, and maybe even in prison. I was trying to find Renato in the dark, so he could grab Pirate and go hide him somewhere. But I could see from the light of the torch that my idiot brother was staring at the cop as if he was an alien. I know just what he was thinking. Mama had smoothed her ruffled hair and gone up to Eunice and the cop. As she walked past, she pushed Renato towards the kitchen, where Pirate was rummaging for food. The two of them could slip out of the only window in the house. Renato took a moment to get the picture. Three seconds later, the light bulb was working. Luckily Renato had already disappeared. I just hoped he wouldn't go and get his mates – I really didn't fancy a shoot-out. By now the cop was chatting with Mama and Eunice. He'd put his gun on the table, a brand new 9mm automatic. Either he didn't notice the mess or he didn't care. I don't think he often got the chance to have a friendly chat with favela folk;

usually it was more like warfare. He showed us a photo of his family. He lived in a favela too, though not a northern one. So we weren't that different. His walkie-talkie kept calling, asking if he needed reinforcements. He just laughed. He was a good guy. He got up in the end, even though you could tell he'd have liked to stay, but that could have made trouble for all of us. As he went he winked, adding that we'd better watch that parrot or he'd end up having us all. Even Eunice was lost for words.

Renato was skipping school more and more often. I couldn't do anything about it, couldn't even judge him, really – he was slipping into the system, and I had to accept it. He had chosen his side. Above all, he was my brother, and there's nothing more sacred than that. He disappeared at weekends to get his kicks at the funk balls. Eunice and I used to worry for him because he was still skinny and not that tall, and at some of the balls there were awful fights between rival gangs. We knew, because the funkers often ended up at the hospital. I couldn't imagine Renato there. Sardine and Chiclete assured me that he didn't dance; he just sold home-brewed beer made by two of his girlfriends. They said he sold about three thousand a night, he was snowed under. I couldn't believe it. He must have made a shed-load of cash – not that we ever saw it. Eunice had offered to act as his bank, but he didn't want to know, so she supervised me instead. I brought in a fair amount of cash and was trying to get my builder and mechanic friends to help me fix up the house. We fiddled the water and electricity meters, and then we started work on a second floor. The Philosopher had given us the go-ahead to build a new storey, which meant we would have three rooms. Eunice didn't think much of all this spending; she advised me to put the money aside for my mother and sisters. She was right, really, and I used to listen to her – until that famous evening.

It had been a hard day, and I fancied a quiet night in front of the TV. When I got home, the pastor was sitting at the table like some kind of Biblical king, in my place, stroking my favourite sister Taissa's hair. Mama had put on a new dress and lipstick for the first time since we'd come to Rio. It all seemed a bit suspect, but I kept my mouth shut until Pirate started singing 'coucouroucoucou'. That ill-omened bird was getting on my nerves, and the pastor kept laughing. Pirate was delighted to have a new audience, so he sang some more. The traitor even perched himself on the pastor's arm, purring. When I went to put him in his cage, the pastor shielded him with his other arm, and an envelope of heavy-duty banknotes fell to the floor. A small fortune. Pirate went for the notes. Mama and Eunice were red with shame but I couldn't see what all the fuss was about, until I noticed that Eunice was still too scared to look at me. Then I understood. It was my cash. My savings, for my future! I wanted to smash the place up, and I don't know why I didn't. I left the house thinking I would never come back. I was so mad that I left without my headphones and the new MV Bill CD, which would have calmed me down. Instead, I went off to find Sardine and Chiclete.

It was all that bloody pastor's fault. If I hadn't come across him sitting in our house with his ridiculous grin, I wouldn't have smoked. Sardine and Chiclete had been teasing me about it for a while, but what those two idiots didn't understand was that when you work in a fucking clandestine hospital you don't get high. And even if you smoked ten joints you wouldn't, because reality would bring you down. But those boneheads were lookouts in zones 3 and 4, and used to smoke while they waited for something to happen. And because Widow's Hill was quiet, they smoked like maniacs. So when I arrived in such a state they took advantage. We waited for the other lookouts to take over, and then went to a dealer to stock up. Sardine got hold of a bottle of *cachaça*, and we took it with us to the top of the hill. Just the view was enough to make us high. Tijuca forest behind us, and in

front the classy condominiums of Lagoa with their swimming pools and tennis courts. Not to mention the Christ
figure perched on the top of his mountain. When I saw the
Christ it reminded me of that bloody pastor. I snatched the
joint out of Chiclete's hands and lit it. The other two
watched, trying not to crack up. I took a drag and almost
choked. Sardine and Chiclete nearly died laughing. I was
dragging on the joint like a madman, but I still didn't think
much of it. I was the Doc and I wasn't high. I got hold of
the bottle of *cachaça* and drank the lot in half an hour.
Sardine and Chiclete couldn't believe their eyes, and they
were pissed off because there wasn't a drop left. I felt all
jumpy and I was fed up seeing that Christ above my head,
with his arms open wide as if he were protecting Rio with
his stone biceps. Christ was doing a shitty job, and I hated
him for it. I needed to let off steam. Sardine and Chiclete
got their guns out. Not their work guns, the others, the ones
they'd won in the lottery. They offered to buy me my first
gun – you could get a decent one for a hundred *reals*. After
that we could go and fire on the wall near the forest, where
the executions were done. Sardine and Chiclete doubted
there would be anyone there. We found a gun. I made sure
it was visible between my shorts and T-shirt, and we headed
off for training. We were stoned, and we got lost at least ten
times – the alleys seemed to go in every direction, and in the
state we were in we didn't know which was which. When we
finally got to the execution wall, a guy was begging on
bended knees. That sobered us up pretty quick, and we
turned straight around. But the bastard, who was about to
die had seen us, and he yelled to us for help. Sardine and
Chiclete bolted like rabbits, but I couldn't run properly
because of all the *cachaça*. The gangsters caught me. They
saw my gun and said, 'You do the honours, kid.'

When she saw me come in safe and sound, Mama muttered
something like, 'The pastor saved him.' Pirate was circling
round above my head as if he were examining me. I pushed

him out of the way and went straight to the shower. I stayed under the water for hours, and by the time I came out, someone had taken my clothes. I looked for them everywhere but they had disappeared. I put on some others and suddenly I saw it. There was blood all over the house, glaring red marks on the floor. Mama Lourdes and her curses came back to me: I could almost hear her gravelly voice. But luckily it was just Pirate. He had got hold of my T-shirt, and then gone and swept his bloodied claws all over the floor, the walls and the kitchen table. I cursed the day I brought him home. Thank God, Mama was getting the kids ready for school, so it was Eunice in the kitchen. She was staring at me in the most awful way, not saying a word. That was the worst, because Eunice always had something to say. I cleaned everything up as quick as I could and had only just finished when she asked me if I was going to work with her or not. I nodded my head and followed her quietly. Pirate said goodbye ten times over, and then Eunice and I saw him right in front of us in the road. He had my headphones with the MV Bill CD in his beak; he could tell that something wasn't right. I hadn't wanted to listen to my CD that day, because MV Bill wouldn't have been very impressed if he'd known what I'd done. He rapped for kids like us, to stop us falling into the system – and here I was, breaking records. The guy at the hospital had given me two years before my first cartridge, and I'd managed to go one better. But the thing that bothered me most was that I hadn't felt any fear. I pulled the trigger, the guy fell, I threw down my gun and I left. Sardine and Chiclete had hidden in an old abandoned shack and came out when they saw we were no longer in danger. They replayed the scene again and again, but all I wanted was for them to shut up. I spent the morning in my dispensary, and the hospital routine calmed me down – I was the Doc and I liked making people better. At about five in the afternoon I was sent to an emergency at the top of the hill. I was pretty surprised, because we didn't go up there often; it was where The Philosopher lived. They let me straight through the roadblocks, and guys were punching me on the arm as if they saw me every day. I went into a house. Some well-dressed little kids, masses of space, and a blonde woman made up like a princess. I recognised her straight away: she was Gilda, one of The Philosopher's women. She gave me a big hug, to congratulate me. I thought she was talking about my work at the hospital, but then I realised that wasn't it. When I finally managed to escape from her perfumed arms, I saw The Philosopher. And right behind him, the pastor.

I had never seen The Philosopher, and I got a big surprise when he stood up. I couldn't understand how such a little guy could run half the northern district. He smiled then; he must have guessed what I was thinking. He had the most incredible smile. Like a TV star. Very straight, sparkling white teeth. Wild. He should have gone into politics with a smile like that – people couldn't help but vote for him. He laughed and then told me to sit down. I was completely bowled over – first of all, because I was in his house, but also because he didn't look anything like a drug trafficker, and even less like someone from round here. But he was born and had grown up right here in Widow's Hill. On the walls were a huge poster of a soldier in a beret, black and white photos of Rio, and books. Books everywhere. Enough to make you dizzy. Eunice would have said it couldn't have been very practical, what with the dust. My first thought was that reading so many books must give you a headache. The Philosopher was looking at me, and it felt like he was right inside my brain, and I couldn't think a single thought without him knowing it. So I just stared at the poster. The Philosopher told me who it was. His name was Chi, or Cho, or Che something, I can't remember exactly. Anyway, the guy was dead now, but he'd fought for people to have a better life. The pastor was nodding, and that really pissed me off: the two-faced bastard. So, this guy with the beret was sort of like a military MV Bill, I reckoned. The Philosopher found that very amusing. The bloody pastor said he had also come here to help the poor. His patter made me want to throw up. He gave thanks to God every day for having landed in a favela with such an intelligent, reasonable boss. Between them, they would make Widow's Hill a model favela. God would help and protect them. That pastor was really going for it. Even The Philosopher forked out. I couldn't believe it. I noticed there were no weapons in the living room. How could you be a boss and not have an AR-15 at your side? I was really impressed by The Philosopher. I was even starting to like him better than MV Bill. He asked me questions about my work at the hospital and kept saying how useful I was to the Widow's Hill community. Community – yeah, right. I worked so that my family had food on the table, but he didn't need me to tell him that. Then he talked about Renato, said that he'd been hearing about him. I swallowed hard – the nice bit was over. I wondered what Renato had been up to now. Apparently, as well as brewing beer he dealt a bit, but bypassing the proper networks. The only reason The Philosopher hadn't shot Renato's hand off ages ago was out of respect for me, my mother and Eunice. I saw him look at the pastor when he said 'your mother', which I didn't like much. But it wasn't really the moment for a show of jealousy. The upshot was that I'd better talk to Renato before he got into some serious trouble. The Philosopher wasn't smiling now, and I suddenly understood how he ran half the northern district. The pastor was reading his Bible, but I could tell how chuffed he was to see me freak out. The Philosopher got to his feet – the interview was over. He took a book off the bookshelf and gave it to me, as a present. I made out I was really pleased and headed for the door. I wanted to get out of there. The day had been a little too eventful, and I was a bit unsteady on my feet. The Philosopher walked me right to the front door, and before he let me go he said, 'Don't you mess around with guns any more.'

The real grief started not long after that visit. Renato had listened to me with contempt. His goal in life was to be like Elias Maluco, the boss of the neighbouring favela. Elias Maluco was famous for his torture techniques and the countless murders he had committed. He was one of the most feared men in Rio de Janeiro state. Renato said that he was a real boss, not like The Philosopher, whom he hated because of his ideas about peace and reform. One night, Renato gathered up his things and vanished. He must have gone over to Maluco's zone. Eunice and I gave him about six months. God only knew if we'd ever see him again. What were we going to say to Mama? Pirate was so upset he didn't eat for three days – Renato was always whacking him, but Pirate worshipped my brother. He just stayed in his cage whimpering, 'Toto, Toto, Toto', all day long. Even the girls couldn't cheer him up. In the end I got so sick of it I put my headphones on his head, with MV Bill playing – it was bound to do him good. But instead of learning the songs Pirate bust up my headphones, and I had to get a new pair. That wasn't a good period. And what's more, Eunice had decided I was going to be a doctor. A real one. With university degrees and everything. She and Mama had decided I should go to school. The only words I knew how to read were the big colourful ones on the pill bottle labels. Eunice taunted me that such ignorance at my age was a disgrace. The Philosopher had given me a book and I couldn't even read the title. She went on and on about it – she must have repeated the word 'disgrace' about ten times. In the end I told her that what was really a disgrace was to be so fat and eat so much. And to have taken my savings and given them to that pastor. That was disgraceful. I was angry. She had hurt my pride by showing me the youngest ones' school books, with their tidy writing and good marks. But there was nothing at school for me; I wasn't going to hang out with five-year-old kids. I was the Doc. I had a reputation to protect. Eunice pestered me every day, and in the end she got me. MV Bill had a concert coming up. She offered to get us both tickets – her treat – if I agreed to take lessons. I laughed my head off – the thought of fat old Eunice at an MV Bill concert was pretty funny. Mama said she'd found me a private instructor, so my reputation would be safe. I was really happy. I knew that MV Bill and Gringa would have been proud of me making such an effort to go straight. So I said yes. I bought a notebook and some pencils and hid them in my meds box, so that Sardine and Chiclete wouldn't see them. Then I went to the address that Mama had given me, and I almost had a heart attack – it was that fucking pastor. That was the end of my thirst for knowledge. I was about to go mental like last time, but then I remembered what had happened and calmed down. The pastor was bare-chested, wearing shorts and flip-flops: favela uniform. He didn't seem so intimidating this time. Even his voice was different, softer. He seemed like one of us. I was just about to fall for it when I remembered those envelopes stuffed with cash, Mama's wedding ring and the ten per cent of their salary that his moron congregation gave him every month. But that wasn't the worst. I don't know how I could have forgotten the most important bit: Sardine and Chiclete had told me that people gave him their glasses and even their gold teeth. Apparently, Jesus would give it all back to them later. Sardine and Chiclete took the piss, saying that the Universal Church of the Kingdom of God was the business of the future. And a great way to get girls. It seemed that the pastor had quite a few . . . But then Sardine whacked Chiclete to shut him up. Chiclete had forgotten that the pastor took Mama to the cinema. They changed the subject and started talking about the big boss of the Universal Church of the Kingdom of God – a bishop, absolutely loaded, who owned a TV channel, radio stations, an aeroplane and gorgeous houses all over the world. If you're going to steal, it's better to be a trafficker. At least then you're honest and upfront about it. Anyway, I was thinking about all this at the pastor's front door, and he was getting impatient. I told him that I'd changed my mind and I didn't want anything to do with his lessons. He said that Mama would be very disappointed, and then I felt like slapping him. How dare the bastard mention my mother! He was asking for it. I had controlled myself all this time because Mama had started smiling and singing again, but this was going too far. I swung him a right hook you-know-where, Mike Tyson-style. Shame Sardine and Chiclete weren't there to see it. That coward was so shocked he didn't even hit me back. Before I left, I told him never to set foot in our house again. He could forget about my mother, and if he dared to come near, I'd go and complain to The Philosopher. The pastor went bright red and swore he'd make me regret saying that. I left him blabbering and went off to the hospital. When I left work that evening, a military police van was waiting for me. What a coincidence.

There were three of them, hiding behind their balaclavas. I couldn't see their faces, only three pairs of eyes, clearly excited at the thought of what was to come. Everyone knew that the PM made extra cash by bumping off kids. They called it clearing vermin from the pavements. Sometimes you only had to give them the bullets and they'd do it for free. The favela wasn't their usual territory; they only set foot here for a good reason. I knew straight away that this was the pastor's doing. God's servant was buying me a trip to hell, and afterwards he would go straight to console my mother. They caught hold of me by the scruff of the neck and threw me on to the back seat. Just to talk, you know, to ask a few questions, nothing to worry about. Well, they sure made me feel safe with their balaclavas, their guns and their beery breath. The radio was blaring and I listened to the music to blank out the sound of my heart thumping in my ears. I knew the song; I definitely knew it but who was the singer? It was a heavy rap, one of those you hear once and can't forget. The bass filled my whole body, and the rhythm merged with the beating of my heart. My mind was empty, my hands were on my knees and I was staring at my fingers to stop them trembling. They started insulting the singer, calling him a dirty ape, a bloody nigger, fucking MV Bill. I looked up. MV Bill. MV Bill was there with me. I had been freaking out so much I hadn't clicked. If I'd believed in God I would have taken it as an omen, a sign that I'd get through this OK. We'd been driving for a while, and I just wanted to get it over with. When we finally came to a stop there was no noise at all, just stink. The reek of dead animals, of decay. We must have been near a rubbish tip. Very practical. They got me out of the car and I threw up. Right on one of their boots. The first punch came and I went down. I had decided not to put up a fight, to just give them what they wanted. That was my only chance. I begged a bit and blubbered for real. I thought of Mama Lourdes: the old witch was probably watching all this in her crystal ball. I got a sudden flash of Gringa and me sitting on the church steps, but that made it hurt even more, so I tried to switch to MV Bill. His lyrics gave me strength, but the cops' insults were worse than the pain, the fear and my helplessness. Hate came over me, flooding my body. It had always been there, tucked away. It came back like a huge wave, and I drowned. My face was pissing blood and I could hardly breathe – only hate was keeping me alive. I had to hold on. For Mama. For the little ones. For Eunice and the MV Bill concert. To see my Gringa again. To get them back. The cops stopped. Job done, they thought. They were sweating so much they'd taken off their balaclavas. In any case, there was nothing to fear: they'd finished me off. Hadn't even needed a bullet: I wasn't worth it. The biggest one wanted to go, because of the stink. The other two said no, they wanted to have a smoke first. A nice smoke, like after sex, the guy said. They had a laugh at that, opening the boot and sitting on the edge of it for their smoke. They even had beers. The punch up had made them thirsty. I was lying at their feet, a few inches from their military boots, and they were chatting away about what they were going to do with the pastor's cash. A new TV, holidays. They prodded me and drank to my good health and that of the pastor. I wanted to see their faces. I opened one eye. It was a bit dark, but the lit end of a cigarette helped me see one of their profiles: a fat guy with a wart on his nose. I closed my eyes again. I knew him. He lived about ten metres from our house and always said that he was a taxi driver. His wife went to see the pastor with Eunice and Mama, and he used to come and eat at our house on his days off. That same fat, warty man was smoking right next to what he thought was my corpse.

When the pastor saw Eunice coming, at nine that evening, he thought I'd been found dead. He put on a suitably sorry face and went up to console her. Eunice had simply come to get me; she couldn't understand why he was trying to take her in his arms. And anyway, she was so fat it would have been impossible. The pastor told her that he would take care of the funeral arrangements, and that the Universal Church of the Kingdom of God would pay. Eunice wanted to know who was dead, and there was an embarrassed silence. Eunice asked again, and again the pastor didn't reply. Everyone knew that Eunice wasn't kidding when she slipped into her Fortaleza accent – and anyway, at one hundred and twenty kilos, with her eyes full of rage, she was pretty scary. The pastor knew her as meek and mild, from Mass. That day he thought he'd seen the devil. He got down on his knees, but still didn't say anything. Eunice was yelling for me louder and louder, and he just stayed quiet, looking at the ground. To tell the truth, Eunice already had doubts. MV Bill and I had finally got her thinking about her pastor and his racketeering. She couldn't understand why she was supposed to give all that money to the Universal Church – Jesus didn't need prime steak! So, Eunice decided that he had better confess fast. She was yelling so loud that the neighbours came over. Tutu the carpenter was there, Clelia the dressmaker, Tasso the driver, Zeca the barman, Galileu the painter and even Sardine and Chiclete. The whole gang – a bit like at the Square. The pastor made up some bullshit about me wanting to leave Widow's Hill to try and find MV Bill. Eunice didn't believe him, and nor did the others. I was the Doc and I would never have left without saying goodbye. In any case, the MV Bill concert was just coming up, so he was definitely lying. Then Mama arrived, brought by radio favela. She planted herself in front of the pastor and waited for him to say something. She must've been sick of losing her kids, because then she did something unbelievable. She took Chiclete's gun and held it to the pastor's head, telling him that now was the time to pray. Sardine reckoned our family must have a knack for killing people – to him, having some kind of family execution style was really class. Except that Mama didn't kill anyone, because the pastor ended up confessing. Everybody was so shocked that they just stood there like idiots for a moment, not doing anything. The pastor took advantage of this and ran off, but Sardine and Chiclete caught him. They were totally proud. Then, The Philosopher turned up to sort things out. No one had ever seen him so angry. His right-hand man, Mandarin, went to the fat warty guy's house. His wife started screaming, so Mandarin shut her up with a bullet through the heart. Then the warty guy turned up, singing and drunk, his T-shirt still covered in my blood. His wart started quivering when he saw his wife on the floor and Mandarin on his sofa. He barely had time to realise what was going on before he joined his wife in heaven. Then Mandarin met The Philosopher at the execution wall for their little theatre production. The Philosopher had decided to make an example of the pastor by having him repent for two days before sending him to the devil. They had him on his knees against the wall, in the middle of a circle of candles bearing the insignia – that bloody dove and heart thing – of the Universal Church of the Kingdom of God. If he let himself relax for even a second, the pastor would burn to death like a saint on a stake. He begged for mercy as he knelt against the wall, stiff as a rod. Everyone in Widow's Hill flocked to see him. It was like a procession, except that instead of receiving praise he was bombarded with insults.

As for me, at that point I was in a coma at the rubbish dump. The rats were having a field day with my injuries – Chiclete swears he shot them one by one without touching me. I don't really believe him, but still, it's a sweet thought. Then I was back in the clandestine hospital where it had all begun, with Eunice groaning over my cuts. Except that this time the mattress didn't stink, the faces around me were familiar, and I wasn't scared. I even had Pirate to keep me company, imitating Eunice and her weird habits. I was doing fine. Gringa had sent me a card which Mama kept reading to me, over and over. The Philosopher had sent me books and a huge poster of MV Bill dedicated to 'Doc'. I had asked The Philosopher a favour: to let me shoot the pastor myself. He refused, saying it wasn't a job for me. Sardine and Chiclete thought that was a bit harsh, and I wondered whether Eunice hadn't had something to do with it. As if he knew how disappointed I was, The Philosopher arranged for me to have a couple of minutes with MV Bill in his dressing room after the famous concert. It was the best day of my life. Even Eunice couldn't get over it – I saw tears in her eyes. MV Bill was so cool. He asked me to write about my life in Widow's Hill and said he would make a song out of it: a present for my tenth birthday. We shook hands, and I swore to him that within two months I would be able to read. It was magical. His people drove us home. Waiting there, in front of the little red door, was Renato's body.

SÃO PAULO

Ivone querida,

Thank you for your letter, which I got just after the funeral. Sorry for only replying today, but I'm so weary. I should have listened to Sergio and never left the Square. Everything that's happened is my fault; all I can do now is accept it.

Sergio organised everything, with Eunice's help. Eunice is a wonderful woman from Fortaleza who has taken us into her home. My only consolation is that the little ones don't seem to have taken it too badly. But as for Sergio, he has changed out of all recognition. All he thinks about is avenging his brother. He's convinced that the gangster Elias Maluco killed Renato, and now he and his mates Sardine and Chiclete have sparked off a series of revenge killings between our favela and Maluco's. If hell exists, this is it, Ivone. All the little coffins going past, the weeping mothers and this fear. We should never have left the Square, never.

God alone knows what the future has in store for us. The Philosopher wants us to leave Rio because he doesn't think he'll be able to protect Sergio for much longer. He's found us some-where to live in São Paulo. I don't know what life will be like there, but it can't be worse than this. Ask Father Denilson to say a Mass for my babies; ask him to pray for them and for us too. You might even have to visit Mama Lourdes and ask her to get rid of this curse. And look out for my Sergio – you wouldn't believe how he's grown up. Even his Gringa wouldn't recognise him.

Ivone querida, *I hope this finds you well and that Turco is being good to you. You deserve it. You'll find my address in São Paulo overleaf, and here's a ten* real *note for the Mass.*

Yours ever,

Antonia

Ivone holds the missive in both hands and re-reads it. Her tears flow, the ink runs all over her fingers, the writing starts to fade, the sentences become illegible. No sooner has she smoothed out the paper than it folds again, as if to enclose its bad news. Ivone crumples the letter in her clammy hand, squashes it and throws it into the distance. She remembers Antonia standing at the bus station with her children, radiant at the prospect of leaving Salvador. Ivone envied her then, but today she is exasperated. No one will stop her from leaving. She is so close now, she won't let herself be weakened. Not by this letter, not by Turco, and definitely not by her mother.

Ivone looks around coldly at what, before, used to seem like paradise. A run-of-the-mill cafe, a few redone houses, an over-ornate basilica and a sky-blue church. The Square no longer touches her heart. Before leaving she will have a Mass said for Antonia and will make sure that everyone attends, whether they want to or not. As for Mama Lourdes, the old witch will do nothing without pay – they'll have to organise a collection or get hold of a case of *cachaça*. She'll see to it. Later. She doesn't have much time right now; she's not allowed to leave her post without the canon's approval. Having to beg for privileges is as much of a strain as the heavy silence of this ageless convent. She has to leave. To go far, far away. And this time nobody will stop her. She's already wasted enough time in this moth-eaten back of beyond – she deserves more. She would have packed her bags ages ago if it weren't for her Pipoca. Ivone smiles; here he is – walking towards her with his doddery gait and worn-out, ageing body. She feels a twinge of sorrow, and suddenly all her strength flies out the window: she doesn't know how to tell him what she has decided. Arm in arm, they walk into Father Denilson's church. The statue of Nossa Senhora de Aparecida welcomes them. Ivone finds the saint's eyes hard and unforgiving. She remembers Maria Aparecida's words: 'Away from the Square you are nothing. You are too beautiful, and beauty brings misfortune.' Ivone lets go of Pipoca's hand. The coloured candles are blinding her, the walls are spinning, the heat is making her dizzy. She is suffocating. She must go. Now. Right now. She can't stand this bloody Square. Enough. He'll be fine. She'll leave tomorrow.

The bus is full to bursting, its tired old frame creaking. Its small scrap-metal belly is loaded down with mangos, papayas, bananas, beans and tapioca. Litres of *cachaça* sway indolently in their beautiful transparent bottles. People get on, others get off. A child starts bawling; nobody seems to mind. Passionate goodbye kisses, final pieces of advice, discreet tears. A sweet perfume hangs in the air; a blend of sea spray, coconut and melancholy. Ivone observes all the agitation fondly. Pipoca, Gringa and the others had accompanied her, but she's asked them to go. About ten seats are still empty, and the bus won't leave until every place is taken. Outside, a couple and a family are buying their tickets. The bus is now full, and they are about to leave. Ivone can't wait, despite Antonia's words engraved on her brain: 'I never should have left the Square, never.' Those were the despairing words of a grieving mother, nothing to do with her. Ivone shakes off her dark thoughts and starts singing a Gal Costa tune. She pulls down her flowery bag and starts rummaging through it – tidying, feeling for something – and then looks up. Two sad, deeply resentful eyes are staring at her. She becomes once again the shy, clumsy child who never knew how to satisfy this intractable glare. Her mother is standing stock-still, stiff in an impeccable Sunday dress with her hair pulled back in a severe bun. She doesn't wave, or call out. Ivone clings desperately to the old leather seat, gripping the armrest, icy sweat running between her shoulder blades. Suddenly she feels ugly, ashamed of her too-short skirt and too-pink lipstick. In those eyes, Ivone has never been anything but an unworthy little girl. Her biggest disappointment. Her mother looks scornfully at her one last time and walks slowly away. She doesn't look back. The engine splutters, the driver jauntily announces their departure. Some of the passengers whistle. Ivone returns to her place, more determined than ever to leave Salvador. She picks her way through baskets, drums, a few tardy passengers. She'd had to fight for her window seat near the back of the coach. Her neighbour is a smiling, matronly woman who smells of onions and cheap soap. Her cheerfulness and volume are overwhelming – Ivone has to guard her space with elbows and the odd judicious look. She doesn't feel like starting a conversation – no, she would rather curl up against the woman's comforting bosom and forget the frigidity of her mother's arms. But the smell of onions puts her off. Finally, with a jolt, the coach is on its way.

Deep blue eyes stare back at her from the mirror. Olympia appraises her reflection. Is it an illusion, or her mirror betraying her? The blue irises move right up to the mirror and examine it. Sloth has taken over her flesh, fading the fine features and remodelling her face. It won't be long before a younger, fresher girl takes her place. Another facelift, perhaps? Olympia stretches her skin back towards her ears, but even surgery wouldn't do the trick. Too bad. She is tired of this life, of this barren celebrity. Pretending, being nice, faking... The whole game weighs heavily on her. Not a day without photographers, without idiotic interviews and pointless gossip. And the fans: their clammy hands, their blissful smiles, that clamouring admiration. Olympia doesn't exist for them: it is Flavia, Gisèle, Ana and the others that they have loved or hated. All those characters who were nothing like her and whom she'd pretended to be, for her fans. So, just for them, she agrees to play the game one last time. She calls out confidently for her make-up artist, Gloria, to come into the dressing room.

Goodbye, Bahia. Farewell, Salvador! The beaches flash by, endlessly. Ivone pays her last respects to her beloved goddess Iemanja. In São Paulo, there will be no sea. She hugs her large pink bag to her like a suit of armour. It contains her means to survive, what she needs to get away from those furious eyes still haunting her. Years of sacrifice for a change of life. Thousands of tickets sold in that gloomy, tomb-like convent. She'd had enough of that robotic life, tearing off and handing out tickets, eight hours a day, Tuesday to Sunday. The dry sound of a ticket exchanged for a dirty *real*. No more bland tourists, no more sordid propositions and cheap promises. She will miss only Pipoca, her fat old loner darling, so dear to her heart. But thankfully Gringa has promised to look after him. Ivone doesn't want to think about Turco; she holds back her tears. After all, Sergio and Antonia are waiting for her, there, in São Paulo. Ivone will look after her and the little ones. She can't wait to see Sergio again – has he really changed so much? The matron keeps glancing at her, dying to chat. Ivone stares out of the window. Everything will be all right.

Tonight is the concluding scene: it will be her farewell, her final episode. Gloria, faithful companion since the early days, comes in and sets up her stuff. A dozen bottles, pots and compacts invade her dressing table before taking over her face. Conscientiously, Gloria shades and softens, concealing wrinkles, marks and blotches. Her fingers carefully repaint the contours of a face weighed down by bitterness, a face she knew when it was young. Olympia watches her work. Her movements are quick and deft, tender almost. She puts a hand on Gloria's arm, stops her. Gently, she pulls off her headband and shakes out her long blonde hair. Next to the hairbrush, a pair of nail scissors. Olympia picks them up. Enough of this lacquered, perfect hair, copied a thousand times. One by one, the locks of hair fall on to the dark carpet. The scissors keep going: small golden bundles land all over the dressing-room floor. A grip knocks at the door. The director is waiting for her on set.

Ivone has promised to write. Father Denilson immediately

offered to teach Pipoca the basics of reading. It will mean going to the church every day for lessons; but he misses his darling so much he's willing to make this huge sacrifice. He sighs. The Square is changing, emptying. First Maria Aparecida, then Sergio and now Ivone. When will the next person leave? Maria Aparecida had her faults, but she knew how to keep her people together: the Square flocked around its queen. Now even Rubi and Safir have lost their chirpiness. Pipoca is looking for Gringa – they must take things in hand, give the Square back its old vigour. He stares at the basilica clock: the two hands are in a vertical line, so it must be six o'clock. The bus will have left Salvador, taking Ivone to another life. With a heavy heart he heads for Father Denilson's church. Gringa is sitting on the steps, humming. She smiles and hands him a parcel, a present from Ivone. Delighted, Pipoca nervously rips open the wrapping, getting all caught up in the tape and ribbon. Quick, he wants to see. He is sheepish as he turns his present over and over in his plump hands. An exercise book and pencils...

Every foot has a story, Senhor Carlos. Really! You don't realise what people reveal about themselves through their shoes. Sure, you have to know what you're looking for, but anyone can learn that. It took me, Vava, at least two years to really get the hang of it. It's been thirty years now that I've been shining shoes, and I've come to the conclusion that it's a noble profession. Yes, noble. N.O.B.L.E., Senhor Carlos. Let me explain. I add the final touch to the client's image – I make him more attractive, you could say. Sometimes I even give advice – on types of shoe, colour and design. See what I mean? Perhaps I'm too talkative today. Forgive me, Senhor Carlos – as you well know I'm not usually like this. We've known each other so long. This time it's on me. What do you mean, you don't accept? Go on, see you soon, and greetings to Dona Denise.

The bus trundles along, heading inland. Far from Iemanja

things seem more hostile. Her neighbour has curled up against her blouse, her head on her shoulder. Ivone tries to push her off, but she just snuggles up again, sleeping like a baby with her swollen hands clasped over her belly. Oh well, poor woman... Ivone daydreams about Turco's eyes, his body on hers. A kid in front of her has farted; it's suffocating. Ashamed, he hides himself in his mother's skirts. Ivone offers him a sweet and gently strokes his hair. The child gives her a shy smile. In the back row a woman is crying. Ivone feels her pain but refuses to take it on. Luckily, she has her emergency distress-busting kit: foundation, lipstick, mascara, perfume and comb. She takes a quick look in her pocket mirror: her hair is already in full revolt, with stray locks escaping here and there. She should have treated herself to a session at the hairdresser's before she left: lovely tight cornrows with lots of coloured beads. Merry little beads dancing as she walked. Instead she looks like a nobody with this frizzy hair. The matron shifts and snuggles up against her bosom. Ivone pushes her away, pinching the flabby skin with her elegant fingers. It feels good...

Poor Senhor Carlos. With all my jabbering I've gone and chased away my favourite customer. Such an important man, a top TV producer. I don't know what came over me, chattering like that. It's just – you get older. Poor Vava. Vava is the name. It was a client who taught me about good manners. He always used to say, 'Vava, when you don't know someone, introduce yourself and shake their hand.' Well, I can't do that; my hands are all covered in shoe polish, and that wouldn't do, would it? Anyway, the posh guy died, and out of respect I do what he said – except I introduce myself as Vava. Even my wife doesn't know that my real name is Valdémir. But here I am jabbering again. It's not professional. I need to find myself an assistant. I can't cope any more – everyone wants Vava. He works the old way, with homemade products, with discretion. But Vava is getting

old, and so is his back. I've been bending over pe(
for so long, one day I won't be able to stand up.

That Vava is talking to himself again. What a dickn̶e̶a̶d̶.
old guy's losing it. And vain, too! You can smell him three
miles away with all that gel and that naff cologne... And
that apron! Have you ever seen anything like it? Skintight.
Honestly! He's always checking me out and cussing my
shoes. 'Sergio, your flip-flops will ruin your feet.' 'Sergio, in
ten years you won't be able to wear a decent pair of shoes.
Not even Nikes.' Nuts, he is. What the old guy doesn't
know is that I've got a whole stack of smart shoes at home,
but I never wear them to work. A kid selling corn on the cob
wearing shoes worth two hundred *reals* – yeah, right. How
dodgy would that look? I've hardly been in São Paulo six
months, so I'm being sly. I put on my flip-flops, look
wretched and wait for people to buy my corn. But that's just
my front – do I look like a guy who'd sell corn for a living?
My stall is the perfect cover for shifting dope. I keep my
happy pills, my wraps and my white powder right at the
back. Totally organised. I have two kinds of corn on the cob:
the customer chooses either regular or 'special'. I've invented
such a cool trick – see the left side of the ear of corn? I cut
into the top end with my penknife and make a big hole. The
corn is soft when it's been boiled, so it's dead easy. Then I
stuff my little baggies in and close it up again. See? Cool,
isn't it? And if there's a raid, nothing. No one's seen anything, no one knows anything. You might say, just grease
the cops' palms a bit and they'll leave you alone, but some of
them wouldn't be too happy about a kid making more
money than they do... I can tell a customer at a hundred
yards, and I can even tell you what they're using. It's no
accident that I've got my stall right here. This spot opposite
the Globo[6] is gold dust. All the junkies on TV, I know 'em –
the young ones starting out, the smooth old-timers, the

6. Headquarters of Globo TV and radio channel.

sluts. My mother and sisters have been going on about them for years. Poor things, if only they knew. I could get autographs... You should have seen them, these stars, braving the favelas in their bullet-proof cars, armed to the teeth. Don't panic, dear junkies, you've got Sergio now. No need to travel – twenty-four-hour dope service, benefits guaranteed.

Empty. The studio is deserted, a single light bulb flickering. Olympia caresses the floor of the set with her bare feet. She knows every cranny; the warmth of the set has nourished her better than any soon-forgotten embrace. She peers into the darkness, making out cameras, spotlights, cables: faithful companions that it took so long to master, and which she will soon betray. She remembers her first screen test: the cold and pitiless camera, the placid, blinking red eye. She hasn't forgotten her first, faltering attempts, how the star of the day mocked her, the indulgence of the technicians. Glory came quickly, but she wanted more, wanted the big role. The movies have always disdained TV upstarts, so then came routine, automatic pilot, taking jobs for the money. One-upmanship, capriciousness and boredom. Olympia takes a last look round and closes the door; locks it.

Loo break. Ivone shivers in the rain, waiting to use the dodgy petrol station toilets. Idle backpackers keep eyeing her up. She should have worn something more discreet than this flounced skirt; in fact, she should have flown. Unfortunately, she's afraid of flying, and it's expensive, so she might as well stop complaining and just be cool. In the mirror opposite the grubby washbasins she looks drab and tired. For once she doesn't care; she's got plenty of time to doll herself up before she arrives in São Paulo. In the dining room, an ancient TV is showing the seven o'clock soap. Ivone recognises her favourite actor's voice. Today he's due to break off his engagement to the daughter of the rich landowner. The whole restaurant is holding its breath, as is Ivone – far from the Square she has come across a little piece of her world. She's hungry and she doesn't want to miss the last few minutes of the soap. She orders a meat pasty and two chicken ones. Even here, she feels the same anxiety she always feels when an episode draws to a close. She stuffs down her third pasty. As the credits roll, Ivone hums the theme tune, and she's not alone: two of her neighbours are singing the verse with tears in their eyes. The hubbub starts again. She wipes the oil off her fingers and gets out the latest editions of *Quem* and *Caras* – she'll have a little look before going to sleep. That way, her night on the bus will be full of dreams.

Since Ivone abandoned him, Pipoca has developed a passion for the soaps: it helps him feel closer to his darling. He hasn't yet understood all the storylines, but he pays good attention, analysing and comparing them. Soon he will decide on his favourite and never miss a single episode. Pipoca works methodically. He's been watching the seven, eight and nine o'clock soaps. He juggles and channel-hops, keeping to a tight schedule. The Square teases him gently. He lives on the street, so in order to follow all these soaps he sometimes goes to Father Denilson's and sometimes to Nina's. He has to admit that he prefers Nina's because she helps him understand who all the lovers and cuckolded husbands are and what the arguments are about. The priest, on the other hand, doesn't want to know. Pipoca can use his TV, but there's no way he's going to watch such nonsense! Pipoca has a quiet laugh about this. Even the Father has succumbed – he would never admit it, but he always finds an excuse to have a peek. The day before yesterday, Pipoca caught him hidden behind the door. That Father's a right devil . . .

Huge picture windows, white walls, three orchids and a few works of contemporary art. Olympia has arrived home. This house is not even a true reflection of her. Its horrifying quietness echoes with memories of parties full of jealous people. Silence, everywhere. A luxurious prison of deceptive glamour. Olympia isn't complaining; it was she who created the rules. The answering machine shows three new messages: her agent, an ex-lover and a smart boutique. Her life in a nutshell.

The bus continues on its way, calmly traversing the mountains. Ivone's neighbour got off at the last stop. She misses her warmth. The environment is changing – the light seems more aggressive, the hills less rounded, the air heavier. The driver drives differently; you can see the tension in his shoulders. He's got to avoid stray animals, the odd drunk, drivers in too much of a hurry. New passengers board, their faces are shut down, they look haggard. It's five o'clock in the morning, and it's going to be a long, long day. Every day is a new battle to be won. Ivone huddles a little deeper into her seat. In a few hours she'll be in São Paulo.

'Fuck me, this corn thing is a brainwave.' The 'special' corn had been such a smash that Sergio was out of stock by the end of the night. He made the most of it by increasing his prices – the Globo starlets had no idea what things cost, and when they were desperate they forked out. One or two got a bit uptight, of course, but the knife calmed them right down. Between nine in the evening and one in the morning, Sergio made a killing. No competition, and the area was spotless: beautiful and clean. The kind of place he'd move his mum into one day. A nice apartment with a pool and everything... Like the ones he used to check out from the top of the favela in Rio, with his mates and Renato. But in the meantime, better go to the market for supplies. He doesn't have a single cob left. Sergio fingers his notes. Fucking hell, he loves that sound! He counts them again. Not bad for a first night. Definitely enough for a great kite. Kites are his new passion.

Six o'clock, and Vava's stall is already set out. In its usual place, right opposite the Globo. It took him years to get accepted here. At the beginning, the heavies used to pick him up by the scruff of the neck and dump him two streets away; they didn't want tramps by the entrance to the TV studio. They said it lowered the tone. Vava had never been so humiliated in his life. Him, a tramp? Vava was the most elegant guy around. Always clean, shirt starched and trousers ironed. Not to mention the apron, cut and sewn by his wife, a one-off Vava special. A little brilliantine to finish off the look. So, he couldn't bear being called a tramp. It was Senhor Carlos, the famous producer, who saved him. No one dares bother him now. The first employees start showing up at six-thirty, always in a rush, hair still damp, sleepy, with neither the time nor the money for his services. Vava drinks his coffee in peace. His regulars show up later. Vava, the Rolls-Royce of shoeshiners: discreet, not too chatty, great technique. Quick and efficient. The kid with the spot next door hasn't arrived yet. He just rolled up with his barrow a couple of months ago, and the Globo guys didn't say anything. Strange. Vava knows what that means, but he hates to think that this angel-faced kid is already a little gangster.

Vodka on the rocks. Her fifth. Olympia takes a gulp and raises her glass. Chin-chin, sweetheart. Photos of her everywhere, along the corridor, in the bedrooms and the living room. Olympia pays tribute to all these strange women looking down at her. She toasts them, toasts herself, whatever. Her favourite, an outsized portrait, sits on the grand piano. Olympia tears roughly at the silver frame, and press cuttings fall to the floor; adoring articles from another era. Adoring, all right. That journalist who wanted to fuck her... She never did read the critical articles – what was the point? They taught her nothing she didn't already know. She walks into the dressing room. Masses of outfits, sorted by colour, fabric and season. The same exact gap between each hanger, measured to the centimetre. All these racks make her dizzy. She leans on a shelf, in need of support. All these dresses, and feathers, and gloss. Garish colours, plunging necklines, aggressive heels. Olympia is suffocating. She pulls down the hangers, dislodging trousers, skirts and blouses. She rips satin, tears at sequins which, cheekily, twirl in the air before scattering at her feet. Olympia stamps on them, throwing down sleeveless tops, jumpers, vests, her hands rummaging through the drawers bursting with lace and silk. She grabs hold of the shimmering fabric, but it slips between her fingers. A shrill sound rings out, making her jump. She backs into the corner of the dressing room, hides behind the furs, eyes shut and heart beating wildly and – feels like a fool. The answering machine! She heads for the mechanical voice but crashes into a baroque mirror. Her face, lit by the moon, is grey and ravaged. Furiously she throws her glass at the mirror. It shatters. As does Olympia.

Ivone leafs through *Quem* for the hundredth time – she never tires of it. This week there's a special feature on Olympia Wagner, a whole series of articles on her favourite star. She has turned down the corners of the pages where Olympia is at her most spectacular. Her two favourites are at Olympia's country house in Campinas, and at Dior in Paris. The star shares her favourite haunts and a few beauty tips. Ivone smoothes out the cover and slips it carefully into her old pink bag. She'll have that edition for ever: Olympia is her role model.

He has been asking himself the same question for fifteen years. How could he have married her? He is chronically bored. Olympia. Carlos can't stop thinking about her: her elusive perfume, her sudden impulses, the unexpected. Denise: dinner at seven o'clock, Sundays at the club with the in-laws, holidays at Ilha Belha. Denise the banker manages his life brilliantly, with controlling zest. So much wasted time away from her, from her breasts, her mouth. Olympia the free. In that silent, languid, nonchalant house. He imagines each day dawning different, with no children, no constraints. A life without Denise.

Pipoca squints up at the hands of the clock, concentrating. Just after seven: Ivone must have arrived by now. Suddenly he has a nightmarish vision: the thousands of enormous buildings, the violence, and his darling so vulnerable. Pipoca is severely shaken. Since Ivone left he has been watching the TV news and also one of those programmes that shows nothing but disasters: murders, rapes, kidnappings, trafficking, shoot-outs. Half these events take place in São Paulo, where a helicopter criss-crosses the city tracking the crimes and filming arrests, chases and confessions: live blood for the viewers. He watches, fascinated, fear gripping him until he can't sleep at night. The Father got annoyed and told him to go and watch his horror films somewhere else. Nina doesn't want to know either. So Pipoca hangs out with Pious Teresa, who is now looking after the convent. Teresa used to watch only religious programmes, but she has agreed to bend the rules because the end of the world is nigh, and this programme proves it.

The driver announces Vila Matilde, on the outskirts of São Paulo. Favelas as far as the eye can see, heavy traffic, scruffy-looking kids dodging between cars, loaded down with things to sell. Tangerines, dried bananas, chewing gum, crisps. Tasty morsels suffused with toxic fumes, sold by coughing children. Children you try to avoid, out of shame, out of fear of their dirty faces, drugged eyes and often, armed hands that wouldn't hesitate to shoot for the sake of a few coins. They zigzag between the queues of cars, surfing among the trucks, buses and motorbikes. Ivone fishes in her bag, finds a note and thrusts her hand out of the window. But it's too late – the bus starts up again, brakes, starts, brakes, wheels squealing. Her head moves back and forth in a steady beat. Boom, boom, boom. São Paulo, here I come.

Carlos wants to see her. Olympia hesitates; this evening she's not sure. He's like a charming, fickle child, a petty bourgeois with nothing bohemian about him but his shirts. Endearing, but a mediocre lover. She gathers up the broken glass piece by piece, putting it in the palm of her hand. She looks at each piece carefully. She's got to put the puzzle back together again: this glass must return to its place at the bar, with its family. A shard catches her skin, tearing it. The gash is deep, the blood glints blackly, starts to flow. Droplets splash on to the spotless carpet. Olympia stares at her injured finger. She brings it greedily to her lips, licks it, sucks it avidly and then bites at the flesh, wet with saliva and blood. She wants more, wants to punish herself, to suffer agonies of pleasure. The glass of vodka has shattered, but the mirror remains intact. The moon shines on this cursed swing mirror, its light so harsh that she dare not look. The showdown will have to wait, for the time being. If only Carlos would hurry up and distract her.

More and more destinations: Florianapolis, Vitoria, Belo Horizonte, Rio de Janeiro, Buenos Aires, Natal, Montevideo... Tietê bus station is restless, the loudspeakers constantly announcing departures. The city names ring out like a slew of invitations to unknown lands. Ivone lets herself be carried by the crowd, one among a multitude converging on a single goal: fresh air. Snippets of conversations, exotic accents, shut-down faces, lost eyes. Some kids come up to her, sensing easy prey. Ivone swears at them. Her heart is beating hard. Very hard. Footsteps pound the tarmac in a deafening litany. She reels, clutches her old pink bag to her chest and keeps walking, further and further. At last a street, and light. A brief respite. Beeping horns, cars everywhere, brusque people, horrible weather. Fear. From now on Ivone is alone in this gigantic city. Pipoca and the Square are far away. No, she is not alone. Sergio and his mother Antonia are here. But first, a whim: she wants to see the Globo.

A distress rocket tears through the blue sky. The starting signal. Time is short. Sergio clasps his parcel carefully between his legs; its contents are fragile. He runs lights, drives on the pavements. A race against time. Only a few minutes till his long-awaited championship. Quick, faster. Sirens: slow down. Sergio curses. Sweat is running down his forehead, the salty droplets are blinding him. He's nearly there. His thighs are cramping with the effort. The parcel scratches his bare legs, his feet slip on the pedals. He can hear the shouting of the crowd, far away. The moped splutters, exhausted by this sudden marathon. It slows – the hill is too steep. The child screams with rage, flings the machine aside and runs towards the wasteland where the competitors are preparing themselves. He tears off the packaging, unwinds the string, checks the security of the fastenings. He glances over at the others. His rivals are mocking him. The punters are impatient. Let the kite war begin.

The letters are still dancing in front of his eyes, really whirling around. Pipoca is exhausted. He has finally managed to recite his alphabet all the way through. He is terrified of the priest, usually so amiable. The slightest lapse turns him into a pitiless tyrant: it won't take much before he's rapping his pupil on the knuckles with a ruler. Pipoca has well and truly earned his next soap, and Father Denilson watches the one at eight o'clock with him. He says he needs material for his sermons, and that Ivone will soon make an appearance.

Carlos is snoring noisily by her side, eyelids half closed, eyes streaked disgustingly with red blood vessels. On his penis, the veins are blue and purple. When he takes her they grow, thicken, grab at her, suck at her until they explode. She wishes he would leave. No one will ever satisfy this bed, no man will ever warm these stiff, too-white, shroud-like sheets. Olympia pushes aside her pillow and takes refuge in the garden. Again, the moon is her witness, its reflection flooding the pool and lighting up the pattern of the blue tiles. There, in the depths of the water, lies her drowned body.

Wake up, girl, you're in São Paulo. Goodbye to nice manners and all that foolishness. Ivone is trying to stop a passerby. People are shoving her, she's in the way. No time to waste on tourists here – you'll have to get by on your own, Miss Bahia. Do you know how many girls arrive from the north every day, drunk on hope? Go to Anhembi Park, you'll find your sisters there, good for nothing but the game. Ivone doesn't believe these lies. She walks faster. It is raining and sirens are blaring, aggressive and threatening. She crosses the road and stops in front of an old woman. The Globo? Good God, it's the other side of the world, young lady. Take the blue line and get off at Sé station. The underground, girl, the underground. Come on, I'll take you to the platform. After that just get walking and ask someone, sweetie.

Sergio is more focused than ever before. He's still got one opponent to beat: an older, stronger guy. Trickery is his only chance. One of his wings got damaged in the previous round, and the wind sweeps into it, making control of the kite more difficult. His hands are bleeding from holding the string. The crowd of punters is going crazy; they think he's going to lose. His opponent takes advantage of this momentary lapse in concentration to dive on him and strike him again and again. He's trying to make a hole in the other wing. Furious, Sergio decides to use his secret weapon: his emergency magic potion. Something his little brother taught him, back in Bahia, before they left for Rio. He has to win. For Renato. Quickly, discreetly, he coats his string with a mixture of crushed glass and wax. This formidable mixture should enable him to cut through his opponent's string. Not an elegant manoeuvre, but all's fair in love and war. Sergio knows that Renato is rooting for him from up high. He wraps the uncoated section of string round his arm. His flying axe is ready to slash the enemy. Sergio gathers his strength and pitches his kite on to that of his opponent, who fights gallantly for a few moments, but Sergio's attack is fierce and unrelenting. He wants victory. The child tenses his muscles and, with every ounce of strength he possesses, launches his final attack. At long last, the string breaks and the kite falls, lifeless and decapitated. The crowd is shouting his name, offering him beer and congratulations. Sergio looks up to the sky. That was your victory, Renato. He doesn't count the money; he wants to go to examine his badly damaged kite. The field clears suddenly – someone has called the cops. Sergio collects his barrow and goes off to the town centre, hugging his kite to his chest.

The underground. She gazes at the walls covered in adverts, reading them one at a time, committing the names of the fashionable products to memory – she wants to know everything. Half the people alight. Others board. A hoarse voice greets them, accompanied by a guitar. The musician starts up a song, the one she learnt at samba school. Ivone can't believe it. Passengers start to stir, tapping their feet and jiggling their shoulders, some whistling. Trying to remain seated, she drums the rhythm on her seat and exchanges some smiles, then stands up to attempt a few steps. The floor is burning under her feet, drops of sweat break out on her forehead. The passengers cheer her on, some of them clap. She dances, celebrating her arrival in São Paulo. Goodbye, wretched Square! The musician speeds up his rhythm, in time with the train. The windows steam up. The carriage shakes. Another girl joins her. A man loosens his tie and plants himself in front of them. The musician takes round his cap, the coins jingle. Ivone wipes the steam off the window and lets out a cry – it's her station. She kisses the musician and runs off towards the Globo.

Thirty years he's been in the profession, and now he's gone and mixed up the colours. Two tins of polish ruined already – what a waste! Vava grumbles into his beard. There's an endless queue, and he's all on his own. The customers are complaining and leaving. All this bustle is putting him off. A hundred yards away Sergio is snoring. He begged him to lend a hand, but the brat didn't want to know. Now Vava doesn't know what to do. A mixed-race Bahian girl comes up. She smells of the sea. She watches silently while he works, her green eyes full of the sun. What can I do for you? The Globo? But it's right there – you'd have to be blind! How can you be such an idiot? The girl takes offence and crosses the road. Vava puts more effort into his client, feeling bad about his fit of grumpiness.

Olympia is no longer there. It had felt like he was making love to a corpse, all floppy arms and stiff body. Horrible. She seemed weird, like a phantom. Didn't let out a single sigh, just dug her nails into his back, scratching him. Denise mustn't see those marks. He gets dressed quickly. Seven o'clock – dinner starts in five minutes, and Denise will be angry. Olympia reappears, her hand is bleeding. He dutifully expresses some alarm. Five past seven. Olympia reminds him of his conjugal duties. Seven minutes past. His mistress's hazy eyes frighten him; Carlos doesn't understand her any more. She comes with him to the door and watches him leave. Ten past seven.

It's the best day of his life. MV Bill pays tribute to his fans for the umpteenth time and then disappears backstage. The crowd brings the house down, more and more excited, chanting the star's name, demanding another encore. Sergio cheers and jumps around, throwing his cap in the air. Next to him, Eunice is clapping – she too wants more. MV Bill is keeping them waiting, but the fans are still hopeful. They start singing his last rap again, louder and louder. Eunice starts to look impatient and says it's time to go. Sergio gives her his most winning smile, but she frowns; someone has tapped her on the shoulder. She turns around to scold them. A great hulking brute with a hi-tech walkie-talkie says to follow him: MV Bill is waiting for them in his dressing room – a surprise from The Philosopher. Sergio suddenly feels like a little kid – what can he say to MV Bill? Paralysed

with fright, he throws himself into Eunice's arms. She rear-
ranges his shirt, wipes the sweat off his forehead and pushes
him into the dressing room. Sergio relives every second.
He's alone with MV Bill, the singer is talking to him and
asking him questions, but all he can think about are the star's
tattoos and the rings in his ears and all over his fingers. He's
totally high – it's like a dream. But then comes the night-
mare. Renato's mutilated body. His mother's screams. Sergio
opens his eyes and thrusts his hand into the corn barrow.
Time for some meds.

She's never seen anything so imposing – her reflection in the
windowpanes is so tiny and ridiculous it makes her laugh!
The Globo tower is so high she has to step back to see it all.
Ivone has crossed the whole city, carrying her old pink bag
and grease-stained magazines, for this tower. She looks up at
the summit, up there in the clouds. She's determined to get
to the top – yes, soon she'll be up there touching the sky . . .
Two men in black suits suddenly snatch her up and dump
her on the other side of the pavement, just in front of Vava.
This time, she doesn't put up with it: she's had enough of
these arrogant Paulistas who think they own the world.
Ivone shouts and swears and struggles. People stop and
watch. The guards are embarrassed and let her go. She jumps
up, smoothes down her blouse and, with a fury she didn't
know she possessed, lets fly with a final string of insults.

Denise signs the Amex Platinum receipt and clicks her
fingers. The driver rushes up to carry her purchases.
Deferential salesgirls, envious glances – this little foray has
been quite wonderful. With her chubby hand she pushes the
reinforced shop door, sending the little newspaper vendor
flying. These wretched people are so aggravating. She found
out yesterday about her husband's romance with Olympia
Wagner. This time she's got one hell of an opponent –
Olympia Wagner, empress of the small screen. She and the
kids have been riveted to her soap every evening. She'll have

to fight smart, and hard. Her Carlos will stay in the fold: family is the most important thing. And then there's the club. What would she look like? Denise refuses to be the next prey of the dismemberment game she's often played. Until now she has tolerated her husband's misdemeanours – twenty smooth years of marriage come at a price. And look what she's got: three divine children, a superb house in the best neighbourhood, a large country estate, a villa at Ilha Bella and holidays overseas. Olympia Wagner. Never. Carlos is so annoying – he might have chosen someone more discreet. The whole Globo must be chuckling. Soon it'll be in the papers, there'll be paparazzi, her name will be mud. Her standing at the club is bound to be affected – it'll be downhill all the way. Carlos is her children's father, he owes her some respect. Denise is serious: it's time for some action.

The soap comes to an end. It is followed by adverts, and then the Globo news bulletin presented by the golden couple. Suitably emotive faces, fake smiles: the ratings heroes. Pipoca turns off the TV. Enough. The news has depressed him – as well as Brazilian poverty, he's now burdened with global suffering. These bloody soaps are making him soft – these days he cries at the drop of a hat. He's got the god-awful blues and a terrible sensation of regressing to childhood: his homework for tomorrow's lesson is lying on his barrow, unfinished. Pipoca is secretly hoping that Father Denilson will fall ill and cancel the class. Nothing serious; just some flu-like thing that will keep him in bed for three days. God have mercy! He's ashamed to have had such a thought. A nice tub of caramel popcorn should make him feel better, give him the strength to do his daily battle with the alphabet. Those bloody letters have decided to make his life hell. Try as he may to concentrate, they refuse to obey him. They're an army of hardened mercenaries, perched along the lines of his exercise book. What a calamity! To cheer himself up Pipoca thinks about Ivone, his sweet adventurous beauty. Nina has been teasing him, saying he's in love. What blasphemy! Pipoca loves Ivone like a father. So, like a father, he is mad with worry. Still no news. He's tried telephoning Sergio's neighbour in São Paulo – she's the only one in the street with a phone – but nothing. No one has seen his Ivone.

Olympia rushes frantically around the house, drawing the curtains and lowering the blinds. She has to protect herself, to stop these thousands of eyes from invading her privacy. She can feel them staring through the mist, sparkling in the darkness, like curious fireflies determined to grab the little she still has. She walls herself up in her glass fortress and turns on all the lights. The living room chandelier glitters. Olympia reaches up, trying to catch all the little beings trapped in crystalline tears. Her wound has opened again, a drop of blood splashes to the ground. She runs to the kitchen, thirsty. Once there, she forgets about the water. She lays her head on the huge stainless-steel table, strokes herself, kisses her metal reflection. It is coarse, misshapen, terrifying. She brings her hand to her mouth to try and hold back her despair, but it is spreading like lightning. Olympia grabs a knife. A long, keen carving knife, the blade sharpened to cut through the toughest of flesh.

Ivone's hands are covered in butter, her mouth tastes salty and there are grains of corn stuck in her teeth. Sergio watches her devouring his merchandise, flabbergasted. He's not sure if he's tripping or if reality is confronting him with a past he'd rather forget. Ivone is all smiles, hugging him and talking about destiny and coincidence. Sergio is hardly listening – he's got to get rid of her as soon as possible: he can't let her move in with them. She keeps kissing him, going on about how much he's grown, jabbering away. His mother mustn't find out that Ivone is in São Paulo. Sergio won't let her poke her nose in his new business. Sergio won't let himself be overcome by memories.

He waits for the formidably thick, reinforced garage door to open. Slowly, he gets out of his BMW and picks his way between the tricycle, a one-eyed doll and some old, flat footballs. He can hear shouts: Denise is scolding their daughter in no uncertain terms. Carlos takes a deep breath: he doesn't want to get annoyed straight away. His butler, dressed in his ridiculous outfit, brings him a whisky. How many will he need to get through dinner? He puts his glass down noisily on the hugely expensive rare-wood chest of drawers he hates. In the dining room, the servants are already serving the first course. He's got no appetite for playing happy family, but a glance from his wife is enough to make him don his fatherly persona. Denise reminds him of tonight's schedule: society drinks and dinner at that famous French chef's restaurant. She holds forth about who will be there, the gossip in town... Carlos has stopped listening for a while now. Suddenly, silence. Everyone is staring at him, an immediate response is required. He's not sure what. Denise frowns, the servants giggle, the children snort. Carlos stands up, gets his keys and walks out.

Pipoca wanders around the lanes of Pelhourinho. Orphan Gabriela is hustling on the corner, Gringa is out walking with her head in the clouds, and a few drunkards are singing their sad love songs. Father Denilson is always offering him a place to sleep, but he doesn't want one. The truth is he likes trailing around in the night-time quiet, and no longer notices the discomfort of sleeping on benches; his back is quite used to it. His feet take him towards Mama Lourdes's house. The balcony is lit by candles, and the clairvoyant's heavy body is silhouetted against a dirty curtain. Pipoca can hear her singing strange Yoruba verses. He turns around quickly, but the gravelly voice is telling him to come in. Hypnotised, Pipoca obeys.

Olympia is on her knees in front of the mirror, swooning in ecstasy. She looks just like the Virgin. One of those kitsch portrayals in which the Madonna weeps tears of blood, hands raised in supplication. Like her, Olympia wears a veil attached to her loose blue shift. Like her, the imploring hands. Like her, the face contorted with suffering. The knife has done its job with her flesh, cutting through her skin like fire through wax. Olympia scratches herself – scabs have formed, and she's no longer able to smile because her skin is cracking. Her crazed eyes travel over her swollen features. She puts her sticky hands on the mirror. Her reflection, endlessly multiplied, no longer frightens her.

Ivone turns away. Gringa would be so sad to see what has become of her protégé. She picks up her old pink bag and waits for Sergio to finish with his customer. Not a trace remains of the young sweet-seller who used to preside over the Square. His face has lost its baby fat and gained a few scars, his eyes have hardened; he looks like any other street kid. If he hadn't cried out in his sleep, Ivone wouldn't have recognised him. The shoeshine man told her that his name was Sergio and that he came from the north. Sergio had served her the corn as if she were a normal customer, with no feeling whatsoever. When she tried to pay, he wouldn't have it. Since then he hasn't said much and doesn't seem to want to know anything about the Square or his friends. Not a single question, not even about Gringa. When the customer has gone Sergio tells her that he's going to spend the evening here, because he makes a lot more money after nightfall. He'll take her to Antonia's tomorrow. In the meantime, he arranges for her to sleep at Vava's house. He's looking for an assistant. Ivone refuses categorically. Sergio adds that Vava can pull strings at the Globo, could introduce her to his friend Senhor Carlos, one of the big producers. It's a good argument and she agrees – just for a few days, until she finds something else. At the Globo, with any luck.

He's obsessed with that woman – he's become her lapdog. Denise rages to herself: never has Carlos humiliated her as he did this evening in front of the servants and the children. His affairs have never threatened his marriage, but this is a different story. Denise won't let another woman ruin her life – she won't be ousted at her age. A man is sitting in the living room – just the person for getting rid of nuisance friends. An unfortunate accident costs about a hundred dollars. Olympia is bound to be more expensive, but what the hell. A woman without a husband doesn't get invited anywhere, and that's the real problem. Her own life has repeatedly been made a misery by divorcées; such a pain to seat at table. The man is counting the money again. Denise taps her foot; she wishes he would do his accounts elsewhere. The job will be done within a week. Satisfied, Denise dials Carlos's mobile for the twentieth time. The answering service, again. She puts the receiver down slowly. Her time will come.

White light and chrome, electro music, waitresses in figure-hugging psychedelic outfits strolling among the tables, traces of childhood still visible under their make-up. Young bankers flaunt their success: they talk loudly, mobiles ring, millions are traded. A few fashion victims sip Diet Coke, looking moody and checking out their fellow creatures from behind their shades. Clones before cloning exists. Carlos finds the whole thing amusing. He must be old; he's feeling weary again. He tries once more to reach Olympia but can't get through. His mobile vibrates. Shit, his wife. Denise will demand an apology, and that's simply beyond him. Bzzz, bzzz, it's vibrating again. This time it's Olympia. He can hardly hear her; she's mumbling something unintelligible, asking his forgiveness. Carlos is frightened. He hangs up.

The stock is ready, and the Globo heavies have come by to collect their envelope. These 'work permits' are expensive, but Sergio wouldn't be able to deal in peace if he didn't pay. That idiot Vava is the only one who refuses to pay. Sergio has offloaded Ivone on to him in exchange for a few hours of shoe-shining – his mother will never know that her friend is in São Paulo. A great idea flashes into his mind: a way to make loads of cash. Let's see ... He'd have to get Ivone in on it, cajole and flatter her, make her think it would lead to a star-studded career on the big screen. Perhaps even give her a few of his coloured pills ... Such a beauty, his customers would really pay for a night with her. Sergio can already hear the notes rustling in his pocket.

'Death is on the prowl,' spits Mama Lourdes. 'Evil, betrayal, fire, Sergio ... A woman, Ivone, death...' Pipoca picks up the shells and hurls them across the room. Lies. This madwoman wants to frighten him – she's amusing herself at his expense. He has never believed her; why should he start now? Pipoca splashes himself with icy water from the fountain. He needs to get himself in hand; he's changing beyond all recognition. First the soaps and now a crystal ball. It's all Ivone's fault. She had no qualms about leaving him, come what may!

The stray dog passes but doesn't stop. The fat hawker is in a right state, talking and shouting to himself. He smells different, no longer the heady odour of caramelised corn but the stink of fear. The stray dog flees.

The old man weaves through the crowd, nudging people out of the way, pulling her along. Soon the stairs will be the only place left to sit. Ivone is puffed out. Luckily a handsome brown-haired guy helps her into the train. Hanging on to the rail, she watches the suburbs flash past. Hundreds of identical buildings covered in graffiti shouting revenge. Kids playing on the tracks; ghost-like figures sprawled on wasteland, shooting up; tired profiles of women making dinner; the occasional gunshot. Apathy. The overcrowded carriage stinks of sweat, bodies brush against each other, the heat is stifling. Ivone grimaces in disgust. Vava smiles at her sweetly. The grey light of the carriage accentuates his wrinkles. At the next stop she's to get off, quickly. The train will continue through this wretched landscape, spitting out thousands of exhausted workers. On the bus she falls asleep and only wakes at the last stop. Not a soul to be seen. Vava explains about the curfew and the deliveries soon to arrive. Children posted as sentries allow them through. The climb up the hill seems endless. Ivone perches on a low wall to regain her breath. Vava teases and encourages her. They continue on their way, briefly greeting the other shadowy figures hurrying home. Eventually, they stop in front of a mud house. A woman is singing amidst the clattering of saucepans. Dona Candida welcomes them cheerfully, asks no questions, adopts her with a sweet look. Ivone thinks of her mother. The meal is joyful, they get to know each other. Afterwards, Candida makes sure that the washing-up is finished in time for the soap. The two women collapse on to the sofa as the credits start. Vava is already snoring.

Olympia is slumped on the multicoloured tiles of her bathroom floor, playing. She dips her powder puff in scented powder and daubs it on her face. It tickles her nose. She laughs, sneezes and starts again. The powder soaks up the blood, making her skin feel tight. Olympia digs her nails into the wounds: she wants to get rid of the scabs. Her whole body is trembling. She's in pain and would like to sleep. Only morphine could soothe her, but where can she get any? Carlos. He's not answering. Her make-up artist. No longer there. Her maid – dismissed. Friends? She doesn't have any. At the Globo yesterday someone told her about a very efficient young dealer. She needs his number.

His mobile rings again. Shit, can't these junkies ever give it a rest? Sergio cuts the call and opens the door silently. He really doesn't want to wake his mother; since Renato died she barely sleeps. The phone vibrates in his pocket. Sergio answers and hears a woman's voice. He can't understand what she's saying. He gets annoyed and hangs up. She calls a third time, her voice clearer now, asking for morphine. He doesn't have any in stock. The woman on the end of the line is breathing noisily. Sergio smells a rat but decides to take the risk, for a tasty price. The lady accepts but wants her drugs within the hour. Sergio refuses; he needs to sleep. She insists, but he won't budge. Tomorrow morning. Tonight, he wants to sleep. He swallows his meds and falls asleep with dollars flashing before his eyes.

The morning sun shines gently on the massive body asleep on the steps of the basilica, caressing it with warmth. Pipoca's resounding snores are disturbing the tourists eating breakfast not far away. Cesar must do something; his customers are not happy... But they needn't worry, Father Denilson has been called. The priest's threatening shadow falls on the dreamer, disturbing his peaceful rest. He mumbles a few words and turns over in an effort to regain that wonderful warmth. The Father coughs patiently, trying to wake his friend. Pipoca is insensible to such trifles. The priest's indulgence has its limits; he runs off to get his communion bell and rings it in the snoring man's ear. With a lazy hand, Pipoca knocks away the source of the noise, inadvertently hitting the stranger in the stomach. It's too much for one day: getting plastered, being late for his lesson, dropping his book and pencils in the fountain, and now this. Father Denilson, who seldom gets angry, loses his cool and grabs his pupil by the scruff of the neck. Pipoca wakes up immediately, stunned by this wrath. Who could be so angry with him? By now the Father has regained his legendary calm and with a benevolent smile guides his lost sheep back to the straight and narrow.

Carlos has done every bar in town, from the smartest to the most sordid. His breath stinks of alcohol, he's staggering. Where now? He manages to get into his car and dabs his sweaty forehead. A bilious attack is coming on; he needs someone to look after him. Denise, Olympia, any woman –

it doesn't really matter as long as they take care of him. Being so drunk makes driving difficult: he can't find his way and keeps forgetting to change gear. The car stalls and some louts start eyeing his motor, so he picks up the pace. Ah, this looks familiar... He's in front of his house. The garage door is opening, laboriously. Carlos suddenly sobers up. Once on the other side of that thick metal door, he won't be able to leave again. Denise will ensnare him in her maternal clutches. He backs out. Direction Olympia.

The pain is fierce, she needs her morphine. Olympia burrows into her bedclothes – she feels less vulnerable in this woollen refuge. The warmth is comforting, and she simmers there in gentle madness. The man said to wait for morning, but dawn is still so far away. The moonlight seeps through the blinds. The black cloak of darkness terrifies her: it shelters spying eyes – she can feel their teeth on her skin. Her bloodied hands thrash around, trying desperately to chase away all these glimmers. The door bell rings. Olympia screams.

Carlos jumps. What a terrifying cry. Olympia would never shriek like that. Perhaps he has surprised burglars at work? The dreadful scream rings out again. No, it must be a murder. A gruesome murder. Carlos needs to get out of there. He can't play at being a hero: he's got responsibilities. As a father, he can't put himself in danger. His watch says a quarter past five; Denise must be waiting up for him. He goes back the way he came. He's definitely had one too many.

Shit, seven o'clock already! No time to hang around. He's got to get hold of some morphine. He's not really in the habit of nicking from hospitals, but it can't be that hard. Nono will take care of it. In any case, best to leave before his mother wakes up. He's had enough of her silent reproaches and her insistence on waiting up for him every night. Right, so Nono will go to the hospital, and he'll find some sucker to deliver to the mad lady. He doesn't want to go himself;

he can smell a bit of a rat. So, first mission: get hold of some mug to do the delivery. Second mission: buy three kilos of corn. Third... fucking hell! He's got it! He'll send Ivone. Give her a taste for easy money. Vava won't be happy, but he'll have to deal with it. Ivone... What a brainwave.

Sit in a subservient position, hold the foot steady, use the polish sparingly. Ivone repeats the three golden rules of a quality shoeshiner. Body sluggish and eyes half-closed, she struggles to follow Vava's nimble movements. The night was too short; Candida dragged her from her dreams at just before five. She'd never got up so early in her life. She had to get ready in two seconds, and then that insane farce of buses, trains and the underground. Again the jostling, the sad faces, the disgusting smells. Perhaps she should have stayed at the Square! At least there Pipoca used to cosset her, and life didn't seem so hard... Vava spent the entire two hours of the journey explaining the dignity of his mission and the basics of the profession. She'd better find something else quick, or she'd be on the first bus back to Bahia. Customers start arriving. Vava settles on his stool, earnest and focused. Orders burst forth: polish, brush, cloth, cream. Ivone passes the items to her boss, who is as serious as a surgeon at an operating table. Ivone tells herself he's a plastic surgeon undertaking a new kind of intervention, the footlift. Seen like that, the work is far less humiliating. Not a bad start to the day after all. The Globo clock says seven twenty-three.

The flames of hell lick at his tender flesh, the beseeching voices of those eternally condemned to hard labour flood his ears; that good old catholic guilt raising its head again, treacherous and vindictive. Pipoca begs; he can't bear any more – inflicting such torture on a friend isn't human. The Father has been declaiming these Bible passages for over an hour now, as punishment. All for a bender and a lost exercise book! Distraction. He's got to create a distraction before he has a heart attack. Any news of Ivone? The Bible closes, and

Father Denilson softens at last; he too has been worrying. But seeing as we're talking about Ivone, we'd better get on with our lessons. A letter must be on its way, and it would be a great sign if Pipoca could read it himself. For the first time, Pipoca realises that the Father is as much of a fanatic as the saints in his church. He looks up imploringly at the statue of the Virgin and asks her to make his ordeal as short as possible.

Nono arrives with the merchandise and launches into his patter about the risks of the job, dodgy contacts and all that jazz. He's after more cash. Sergio won't haggle with a guy like this – subordinates are there to obey, not to make demands. Nono shuts it. He's not keen on ending the day with a bullet in the head. With the discussion over, Sergio calls the client. She seems as if she's in withdrawal – he can't understand what she's going on about, but he gets her address in the end. Important to check the place out before delivery. It's a top class pad, in a bombproof neighbourhood. No bodyguards at the gate. Cameras everywhere. Loads of cameras; they could probably even get your fingerprint. That stupid Ivone has agreed to deliver – if there's a problem it'll be her that's on the front line.

Ivone doesn't want to miss a single thing. She leans on the taxi window, leaving marks with the warm stickiness of her hands. The traffic is bad, and frustrated horns blare out on all sides. She doesn't hear them; her attention is riveted on the girls reclining on advertising billboards on the sides of buildings. Each more sensual than the last. From their posts on high they spy on each other and check each other out, full of hatred, as fiercely competitive as the brands they represent. Too soon, the giant buildings give way to endless walls. The driver plays guide. Welcome to Bunkerland: this is Morumbi, São Paulo's most exclusive neighbourhood. He is offended by all this wealth, talking about fortresses of fear and defences against the violence of poverty. His chatter annoys her. Ivone forgets him, preferring to imagine herself within the lovely clean walls. A pool, a garden, time to do nothing. A famous lover. She imagines the hidden luxury, the concealed stars and their need for protection. She ignores the barbed wire, the cameras and heavies and fierce dogs. The taxi comes to a stop. Here you are, that's ten *reals*. Ivone tosses him a note and gets out without a backward glance. Her eyes feast on the white gate, the ivy-covered walls, the tiled roof. She presses the intercom, hypnotised. Nobody replies. After a moment's hesitation she rings again, keeping her finger on the buzzer. A distant voice murmurs something. Ivone sings out, 'Delivery.' The gates open.

The effrontery to ring on her doorbell. They must be outside, waiting for her. But she has thwarted their plan by not opening. Victory. What if they come back to haunt her later? Olympia dances in her own blood, staining the white carpet of the living room as she plays at drawing poppies with her feet. Now she needs some black. The paintings – what if she took a fistful from one of those big canvases? No. She scours the empty room with her eyes. The piano. Her greedy fingers run along the keys and the cold hard notes ring out. Their echo makes her dizzy. An aural weapon. She scrapes obstinately at the polished surface of the piano. It shines. The gloss attracts her, and she dives into the abyss of her reflection. Her ear rests on the casing, making the creaks of the wood vibrate right into her, slicing into her flesh. A cry tears into the silence. The intercom. Olympia forgets all caution and opens.

Twenty years of tracking and bugging. Twenty years of swallowing her pride and her rage. His face falls as she sets out the hard facts, unembellished, with photos to back them up. Poor Carlos. He laughed to start with, then denied it, then shouted. Now he is crying, with his head on her shoulder. Denise savours the moment. This is the best feeling in the world; it makes her shiver with delight. She strokes her husband's hair gently. They are due at the club.

Buried alive, a slave, that's what he's become. Rescue me, Olympia. Carlos dials her number but hangs up at the first ring, Denise's words echoing through the white marble bathroom. He remembers her sly smile, the triumphant glint in her eyes that he hates. Help me, Olympia. He doesn't know any more, a voice in his head is telling him to forget. His fat fingers dial the number again. No reply. He'll go over there; he owes her an apology. And if Denise finds out? Carlos gets undressed and stands under the potent jet of the power shower. Opposite him, the mirror he has never dared face.

A garden, flowers wilting in the sun, a perfect lawn, the aroma of freshly cut grass. Ivone is dazzled by this cool luxury. She follows the gravel path, the pebbles getting into her sandals and hurting her feet. Eventually, the house appears. It is magnificent: a modern, angular building with huge plate-glass windows. She walks round it, her reflection multiplied endlessly in the glass. The heat of the midday sun is making her sluggish, Sergio's packet is sticky in her hands. She puts it on the patio table and walks up to a window in search of a little cool. The glass is icy. Ivone leans on it and closes her eyes. Her body relaxes, the cold glass seems to have taken it over. Suddenly, there's a squeal and a high-pitched moan. Nails screeching against glass. Endless pain. Ivone turns around, panting. Two huge eyes are staring at her: a pane of glass is all that separates them. There's a muted crack like something breaking. The door has opened. They are face to face.

Pipoca chews on his pencil. The Father has shut him in the sacristy among the dusty old tomes and the cassocks. Two hours of alphabet study. After vespers there will be dictation, and every mistake will cost him a beer. Pipoca stares fretfully at the blackboard. The garrison is there. The letters form tight ranks, their starchiness annoys him. Suddenly, he has an idea. He'll organise a mutiny, sew disorder in this well-disciplined army. He looks at each soldier carefully and tries to spot the troublemakers. B seems the liveliest, with his paunchy stomach and all-powerful look. S is bound to be servile and overly quick to collaborate, M is ambiguous and versatile. F is outraged, pushing past E, N, O, V and I to warn the colonel. Pipoca bends over his exercise book, making a list of the deserters. He has rallied eleven soldiers, with T in charge. Disorder is rife, Colonel L calls the troops to order. They have sworn their allegiance to the Father; any betrayal will earn them a possibly fatal dusting with a wet cloth. An animated discussion gets under way. The vowels don't take sides. This often maltreated minority will simply align themselves with the winners. The door opens all of a sudden: it's Father Denilson. Stand to attention.

Ivone hasn't returned from her dodgy delivery. Sergio has disappeared, and Senhor Carlos hasn't shown his face all day. Vava waited for them in vain and then took the last train home to his favela. Candida tells him not to worry – tomorrow morning, everything will be back to normal. Vava doesn't believe her. He can feel disaster in the air.

The kite lies dying on the wasteland scrub, covered in gashes. It was his favourite. Black and white with an enormous skull and crossbones, like the pirate flag. Pirate. Pirate. Sergio shuts his eyes. No, he mustn't think about Rio. He picks up his moribund kite and examines it one last time. There's nothing doing: a kid from Burraco Quente tore it to pieces. Nature of the game. He walks slowly across the battleground. It's time to get back to his barrow and his corn on the cob, but first he'll have a quick hit. He gives himself a bit extra today, to mark the kite funeral. Renato made that kite. Afterwards he'll burn the paper corpse and then he'll give that crazy morphine lady a grilling. Ivone never came back. Pity. If she's run off with the cash, he'll kill her.

Red. Dried blood, congealed blood. A ruined face, hair darkened by the wounds. Ivone is so numbed by the sight that she doesn't move. The woman comes towards her. They don't take their eyes off each other. Ivone starts stammering about the packet, and points at the table. The woman hardly reacts. She repeats that the packet is there. A flicker of understanding passes through the blue eyes. The woman contemplates the packet with ravaged eyes. Through the window, Ivone catches sight of the floor streaked with scarlet stains, the frames shattered all over the carpet. She goes in. A shard of glass cuts her big toe, she's startled by the pain but doesn't stop. She needs a towel. In the bathroom, a cracked mirror is splattered with blood. Ivone returns to the garden. Blinded by the sun she can't see anyone and simply follows the sound of water lapping. The woman is there, crouching by the side of the swimming pool, staring at the water. Ivone approaches her, murmuring soft words of comfort. She gently wipes the red marks off the woman's face, taking care as she dabs the open wounds. Little by little, the features become clear. Olympia Wagner appears.

A beggar knocks on his window. An ancient, toothless, skeletal woman. He'd like to run her over. The traffic isn't moving, the woman is insistent. His penny drawer is full. Carlos takes a fistful and chucks them as far as he can, across the congested road. The coins fall among the tyres. The beggar shrugs her shoulders and goes to pick them up. The lights turn green and the cars start, knocking her out of the way. Carlos watches her wild dance through his rear-view mirror and, well satisfied, goes on his way. He hesitates a moment. Olympia or Vava? The shoeshine will cost him only one or two *reals*. Olympia, these days, is prohibitively risky.

Vava sips his coffee. He drinks two or three every morning. His wife makes it for him, at dawn, very strong with lots of sugar. Without her coffees and her love he wouldn't survive.

Every day, he goes off to the front line not sure if he'll make it back. He might get hit by a stray bullet, knocked off for a few cents, or be a victim of police extortion – and that's just the worst of it. There are also the muggings, stock going missing, increasing costs, and the bloody violence. Vava has never become accustomed to this fear of going to work, of smelling his wife's perfume for perhaps the last time. So he needs his quota of hugs and coffee in the morning, otherwise he would never go. He combs his hair, kisses Candida and leaves. Bus, train, underground, then pick up his stuff. The day hasn't even started, and he's already exhausted. Another coffee: got to keep going. Vava sits on his stool and waits. Sergio isn't there. The first customer arrives, sticks out his shoes and opens his newspaper. Not so much as a greeting. Vava doesn't take offence; he's used to it... He puts the money in his pocket and asks the next customer to sit down. Senhor Carlos. So early. Strange. Something must be wrong. Carlos talks about the passing of time, about regrets, family duties and life being a prison. Vava glances up at him discreetly. No, Carlos isn't drunk. Just sad, melancholy, lost. Vava offers him a coffee.

His head spins and he falls back heavily on to the tarmac. He'd got into a fight with some guy from the tournament who wanted to nick his drugs. He hears sirens, brakes squealing, men shouting. Sergio doesn't have time to think before the cops grab him and start beating him up with their truncheons. You dirty rodent shithead. Blood in his mouth. The sound of bones cracking. A tooth breaking. They are shouting, and frisking him. Bingo, they've found the coke and the cash – lots of cash. Makes it all worth while. Fucking hell, what do they want from him? Why him? Sergio is scared to death, he's screaming. This is it: this time he's in for it. Renato. Renato, make them stop, I beg you. A cop puts a gun to his head. It's all over. Sergio thinks of his mother, of Percival and his little blanket, Luciana and her ribbons and Taissa, his tomboy favourite. The cops put handcuffs on him and cart him off. He barely struggles. It stinks of piss in the back of the van. Of terror and despair. How many people have been for a spin in this hearse? Were any spared? How many were shot in the head, right here in the back, next to the 'Civil Police' sticker? Sergio listens to them chatting; they're splitting the loot. His life hangs on their mood. One of the cops turns up the music. They whistle and discuss the singer's ass, trying to decide: shall we shoot him or not?

Her head in the stranger's lap, Olympia lets herself be cradled. She lifts her head. A firm hand puts it gently back where it belongs, in the hollow between the owner's long thighs, which smell enchantingly of vanilla and coconut. The neckline of the dress shows off two round breasts. Beads of moisture form on the skin and roll down her front, leaving a damp trail on the translucent cotton, little flowers of sweat darkening the pink fabric in places. Ivone is focused on the cuts, cleaning them with care. She wiggles her feet serenely in the blue-tiled pool. Solid, well-manicured feet. Olympia lies still, enjoying the warmth of these arms, reminded of a long-ago feeling, a smell from childhood. It helps to wipe out the pain.

Satisfactory. Pipoca repeats the unfamiliar word several times. He likes the sound of it. He now knows his alphabet – not in the right order, perhaps, but the main thing is mastering all the letters. Pipoca puffs out his chest. What a victory! The battle was bitter and the enemy tough. It took many hours of negotiation to persuade lieutenants G, Q, K, W and Z to take refuge in his exercise book. The vowels followed obediently, without any fuss. Pipoca had almost admitted defeat. Leaning against the church wall, he raises a glass with the Father. He's relieved – their relationship had been a bit fraught since he started getting rapped on the knuckles with a ruler for every mistake. The postman greets them and rummages in his bag. Surprise, a postcard. Pipoca tears it out of his hands, ready to decipher it. He is soon disappointed – it's a card from the Square, congratulating him on his hard work. He's moved by their kindness. Ivone's will come soon, he thinks philosophically.

Carlos offloaded his sadness and then left. Vava concentrates on the shoe: rubbing, cleaning and polishing. The full deal for a good tip. This guy doesn't look generous – Vava bets he won't tip a damn. The client suddenly stands up, ruining Vava's efforts. What's going on? A kid is dragging himself along, looking pretty ugly, blood gushing out of him. He's crawling. There we go: he's down. So much the better, one less hoodlum. The customer starts up about the favela kids: it's the parents' fault, no discipline any more, the good old days... Vava doesn't reply. It's not the kids' fault – the problem is fear, drug dealers, an under-paid police force, corruption. He has a funny premonition and finishes the shine quickly, pocketing the money and running over to look. People aren't going near. They're staying back looking at a lifeless body lying in a sea of blood. A hunched-up child. Two guys flip the body over, disgusted. Vava wipes the swollen face with the wax-covered cloth in his hands. Jesus Mary, it's Sergio. The kid is in an awful state. How did it come to this? Vava carries the child over to his spot. No one knows if he's already dead. They're all betting on it. Ten to one that he's a goner.

Olympia has fallen asleep at last, injured fingers entwined with Ivone's own. The room is looking better now – she's cleaned everything, although one or two stubborn stains have resisted her efforts. She'll have some professionals come tomorrow and get rid of every last trace. No one must know. Olympia will recover. For the moment Ivone will stay at her side – she is needed. She gives her idol a quick, furtive kiss on the forehead. She definitely doesn't want to wake her; Olympia needs rest, and Ivone will look after her for as long as it takes. She patiently disengages her fingers and stands up. She walks around the bedroom, taking in every detail – the lounge area, the pictures, the fabric on the walls and the enormous television, broken now. She could gaze for hours, but what tempts her most is the dressing room. A long, narrow, wood-panelled room just to the left of the bed. Ivone yearns to try on the jewel-encrusted stilettos.

Denise spends her days glued to the television. The news will be on soon. She can't wait to hear the day's catastrophes – Olympia is bound to feature. She stiffens, thinks. Surely the channels would interrupt their programmes – broadcast a special announcement – for the death of Olympia Wagner? But for now there's nothing. Denise thumps her fist on the table, and a Lalique vase crashes to the floor. She rings for someone to come and clear up the mess, channel-hopping anxiously. Still nothing. But her contact has phoned: the job was done. A servant is picking up the pieces; the young one that Carlos ogles. Denise stands up and – just like that – stamps on her hand. The glass tears her palm to pieces, and Denise feels better.

The sight of blood makes him weak, but this really isn't the time to come over all squeamish. The kid is half-dead: he's got to find him a doctor or take him to hospital. The onlookers have all moved on, their curiosity satisfied, leaving Vava alone. No one is stopping to give them a lift, and he hasn't the money for a taxi. It's not even worth trying public transport. Vava panics, paralysed by the kid's suffering and unable to make a decision. Sergio is emitting little moans, so quiet you can hardly hear. Just enough to make sure he's not carted straight off to the morgue. He's got to hurry: the police will turn up soon, and they'll probably finish the job off. Jesus Mary, somebody help us! The child's face is turning grey, he's giving up the fight, the life is flowing out of him. His eyes, massively swollen from the beating, stay firmly shut. Vava talks to him, wipes his bloody forehead, and weeps. A street hawker has given him a bag of ice to stop the bleeding, but in this heat it won't last long. Sergio is slipping away, his features are starting to relax, to look soft again. A firm hand comes down on the shoeshiner's shoulders. The police. It's all over. He stands up, prepared to do battle. Senhor Carlos is standing there. His saviour.

Her hand is feeling for the light switch when a ray of sunlight floods the darkened room, dazzling her. The light makes a halo around the woman sleeping peacefully at her side, in one of her nightgowns. Olympia stares curiously, struck by the Metis girl's fresh beauty. She is about to wake her up when a flood of images resurfaces. Vague to begin with, but soon becoming clear: the knife, the blood, the pool and then nothing. Olympia rushes to the bathroom and looks in the mirror. The blade has killed the star. She vomits. Olympia is spewing up her life.

Faraway voices float towards him. Angels, probably. Or maybe Renato. Yes, Renato. An immaculate white light floods over him. He must be in heaven! Way cool! With a jolt of remorse, Sergio remembers all the bad stuff he got up to. What will he say to the Good Lord now? It could be a tricky encounter. A fast track to hell. He'll have to say he's sorry and all that jazz... But he knows how to do that. He's got the talk, he'll be able to persuade God to keep him. And Renato will help – he must have some friends round here. Mama, bring me another blanket, please. I'm so cold. An icy cape is enveloping him. It's eating slowly into every inch of his flesh, this flesh of a child grown tough too young. Suddenly Sergio understands. He's not in heaven yet. Too bad, he'll have to wait a bit longer. There's still a battle to fight. The last battle. Sergio versus the Grim Reaper. He's a good sport, he lets himself be beaten. He's got no chance anyway: it's an unequal fight, rigged, fixed in advance. The voices come back, murmuring incomprehensibly. Doctors, most likely. He would like to open his eyes one last time, but the effort is too much. Sergio slides reluctantly towards death.

The bedroom is empty. A sour smell hangs in the bathroom. The blinds are down and the windows are closed. It's unbearably hot. Ivone walks through each room and back again, looking. Where is Olympia? A shadow moves through the kitchen. Ivone follows it but doesn't find anyone. A match is spluttering in the sink. Her pulse quickens: she's got to get out of here. She rushes to the door, but the handle is jammed. She runs into the living room and tries to wind up the blinds, but the power has been cut. No way out. A candle lies on the floor, the carpet is blazing... The fire obliterates the blood-red poppies and rushes towards her.

It's all over, says the doctor. You'll have to fill out some forms, organise the funeral and tell the parents – if he has any parents. Vava and Carlos look at each other, knocked out by all these responsibilities they would rather not take on. After all, they hardly knew the kid. Carlos feels he's done enough already – his BMW is covered in blood, and it will cost a fortune to clean. He doesn't mind paying for the hospital, but as for the rest, it's not his problem! With incredible daring, Vava takes his arm. We can't leave the child all alone in this big cold hospital. Aren't you a believer, Senhor Carlos? We can't abandon the kid like this. They'll dump him into a shared grave like a piece of rubbish. I couldn't bear that. We've both got children. Yes, exactly. It's not my kid. But Vava won't give up. Carlos gets impatient – come on, Vava, stop all this snivelling. Let's go and have a drink: a nice caipirinha will sort you out.

Olympia strolls around her perfectly designed garden. Here too, it's a matter of starting over. She brings a hand to her face. She will probably always be scarred. Carlos will no longer visit. A light breeze blows through the leaves, the fading rosebushes are still giving off their fragrance – a slightly bitter autumn aroma, quite opposite to that of the girl asleep in her bed. Heading towards the house, she frowns. The lights are off, the blinds are down, she can't get into the living room. But she came out through the French door a moment ago. Olympia goes round the house to the service entrance. The kitchen door won't open and the handle is boiling hot. She hears panic-stricken cries. The girl is banging desperately on the plate-glass window. Enormous flames are closing in behind her.

Olympia Wagner's house has gone up in flames. Firefighters are at the scene. No news of the actress. Brazil is on tenterhooks, images of the inferno fill the screen as the cameras feast on this new disaster. Plans of the house are shown, architectural details given, people ponder how much the magnificent villa must have cost. Nina sniffles noisily, not hiding her tears. Pipoca is all worked up – they've got to find Olympia. The camera seeks out the Italian mosaic swimming pool, the French rosebushes, the sports cars. Even Father Denilson gets agitated. Just rescue Olympia!

Denise wriggles about on her sofa. The drama is on every channel, it's straight out of Hollywood. This exceeds her wildest expectations. Olympia Wagner's death, live on TV! She's made a good investment for once. The firefighters have got the blaze under control, but they haven't found the body: it must have been consumed by the flames. Olympia is no more. Denise is jubilant. The area around the charred house is overrun with journalists, the police are struggling to keep order. Questions are coming from all sides about the cause of the fire, hypotheses are advanced. Denise tenses – the mayor is talking about an inquest. There's a knock at the door. It's the man, demanding more money.

The old guy is starting to get on his nerves and the traffic is worse than ever. They've been stuck on the road to Morumbi for half an hour, trying to get to Olympia's house. It was Carlos's idea: an attempt to cheer up Vava, who is angry at him for abandoning the hoodlum at the morgue.

Firemen have cordoned off the area, and sirens are wailing all over the place. Carlos turns on the radio: the presenter's voice sounds serious, but the racket outside is so deafening that he can't hear the breaking news. It becomes relatively quieter, the sirens are moving away. He can hear now. The fire, Olympia. Carlos slumps over the steering wheel. Vava doesn't care – he gets out of the car and returns to the hospital to keep vigil over the boy.

Olympia managed to rescue Ivone from the furnace at the last minute. She holds her up and helps her into a taxi. They must hurry to the hospital – she's worried about Ivone's burns. The taxi driver glances briefly at the two odd-looking women, but he is so excited by the day's events that he doesn't pay much attention. He tells them all about the awful fire and how the famous actress disappeared in the flames. Looks like it's going to be a bad week, he says. Ivone and Olympia don't respond. The taxi drops them hastily and disappears in search of new information. There's a long queue in the hospital reception. Olympia takes Ivone to the surgery department where a nurse asks them to wait. At the end of the corridor, an old man is shuffling painfully along carrying a large box of polishing equipment. He's talking to himself, laying vehement claim to a body. Ivone looks up, recognising Vava's voice. The doctor has arrived, and Ivone follows him for a moment before turning round. She can't see Olympia, or Vava. Far away, at the other end of the corridor, two figures recede and then disappear.

SALVADOR

The fountain that Maria Aparecida so often threw me in is still here, you can smell the flowers in the Father's church from two miles away, and I can even see the strange machine that makes those caramel sweets I love. What's going on, am I dreaming? Have I come to the wrong place? Why is it so still, so silent? Where are the birds? And Nina's cat? Could I have confused this soulless little spot with the Square? Flipping hell! That little female from last night has got me in a right spin – I'm so tired I've gone stupid. I'm going to go round by Mama Lourdes's house: even in this state I'll be able to find her from her sordid smell. But she's not in; it's totally silent there, too. Could I have lost my legendary sense of smell? I'm going to follow my instinct and go up this street. No, I'm not mad, it is the Square – the big jacaranda tree is still there in pride of place. Where are my friends, the gang from the Square? Where are they hiding? Could this be one of their games?

The stray dog gathers himself together, ready to howl like his southern brother, the grey-coated, sharp-fanged wolf. That will definitely get the attention of Pipoca or the priest. He makes an almighty effort and emits a long, heartrending cry, flooded with every ounce of the despair he feels. It threads its way through the walls and under the church bells and finally dies in the fountain, where even the water stagnates. This monstrous endeavour achieves nothing – no one responds to his call. The stray dog's hackles rise, his ears prick up and his tail waves around frantically. Something is wrong. Very wrong.

He heads towards Father Denilson's church, padding cautiously into the nave and following the flagstones towards the sacristy. The scent of flowers is so heady that he gets lost and ends up at the small parish cemetery. A foul greenish froth is pouring into the alleyway; it gets right under his claws. Horrified, he runs back to the church to rinse his paws in the holy water. He would like to bark some more, but not in front of the altar – the God of the humans would punish him. He's got one final hope: Cesar's cafe. The pavement tables are deserted. Not a single customer, just a few dirty cups. Becoming more and more anxious, the stray dog heads for the basilica. How strange: Pious Teresa isn't on the steps selling her rosaries. Now he is sure that the end of the world has come.

Suddenly he hears shouts.

He pricks up his ears. The noise is coming from Cesar's cafe. He goes over and pushes the door, but it won't open. He tries again, in vain. After several attempts he manages to lower the handle by leaning on it with his muzzle.

There they are, all of them, looking at a very big, very strange talking box. The stray dog leaps about in delight, yapping and worming around the legs of his long-lost friends. He can't believe their indifference. He looks desperately for the priest: he at least won't reject him. There he is – he can tell from the clean, pink feet. He dodges in and out of the chairs to rest his happy wet snout against the priest's black gown. His friend is so focused on the box that he doesn't notice the warm and tender breath on his hand. The stray dog's tail droops. Even the priest doesn't want to know. He looks up at this box that has usurped his place and gets the shock of his life!

Ivone. In the black box! A tiny, imprisoned, tearful Ivone, standing in front of a nasty-looking moustached man.

The stray dog makes straight for the box and throws himself against the glass, baring his popcorn-weakened fangs. He wants to set his princess free. There's a lot of movement behind him. He hears a few shouts but doesn't take any notice. A powerful, barely controlled hand picks him up by the scruff of the neck and sends him flying across the room, right on to a crate of sweet potatoes. The stray dog collapses noisily on to the cold tiles, rear-end dislocated and brain more confused than ever.

The priest's chubby feet are in front of him, his gentle consoling voice is speaking. Ivone is fine, and the big black box is a television: a sort of storytelling game for humans. Ivone is an actress. She's going to become very, very famous. Tonight was her first appearance on the box: she wasn't on for long, but enough to make an impression. It's a great honour. The stray dog isn't quite sure he understands, but he's happy. Everything is back in order.

The episode is finished, and Cesar's cafe comes back to life, with everyone chatting nineteen to the dozen. Pipoca is grumbling away in a corner – he didn't think much of the passionate kiss at the end. Pious Teresa is already suggesting a novena to save the sinner's soul. Cesar snubs her, offering everyone a round of drinks: they've got to celebrate their little girl. He gets his best *cachaça* out of the storeroom, to be drunk neat, in one gulp. Mama Lourdes is there in a flash – alcohol makes it easier for her to communicate with the divinities. They drink to Ivone's health, and make bets on her next appearance. Turco is strutting like a cock, talking of joining her in São Paulo and swearing that he'll be faithful – once he gets there that is . . .

Dr Augusto hasn't touched his glass. He hasn't the stomach for that stuff, and anyway, he doesn't know how to tell his friends about Zé and Manuel's arrest.

The last carriage of the express train disappears into the surrounding greyness, a rusty meteor crossing the horizon of those condemned at Canju, the high-security penal colony where eight thousand men languish and rot. Metallic dust blows through the already polluted air. The regional train will come by in half an hour, leaving its trail of greasy food wrappings, cigarette butts and splinters of glass, and then another express. The usual hubbub has given way to a terrifying silence. Silence is never a good sign here. The days lack light, the hours are oppressive and the minutes murderous. On the third floor of Wing 5 one man implores, while another guffaws cruelly, showing no mercy. The wardens watch them through the spyhole and then return to their station at the end of the corridor.

Cell 402. Thirty men in six square metres. They take turns sitting down and have to pay for a few hours of sleep. In one corner a teenager is dying, his eyes turned to heaven in final petition. They've accorded him the privilege of doing it by the window, on condition it doesn't take long. An old guy is fanning the air above his head with a sheet of paper. The single sheet of babyish handwriting has been read so many times it is almost illegible. Manuel recites Zé's words like a prayer. A litany to exorcise fear.

Manuel. This paper isn't very big, so I hope you will be able to read it. Since Sunday's uprising I've been transferred to Wing 7. I've seen worse; The Tuner is in charge – he's fair, and there aren't too many killings. Apparently, it's horrific where you are, in Wing 5. They tell me you're ill, that you've caught a bad flu. Hold on, dear Manuel, I'm negotiating for a bed in the sick bay.

Your own bed, nice and clean, for the first time ever. So hold out and wait for me.

The sheet of paper hangs in the stinking air. Manuel has closed his eyes. The old guy reaches out to touch him – the kid might be dead. Good. More room for the rest of them.

Dr Augusto didn't sleep well, but then he hasn't slept well for years. Not since the dark times of the dictatorship and the interrogations at the military school, and that day when his courage deserted him. Only the sun is occasionally able to subdue the cries of those who were able to stay silent. He opens the shutters wide – the narrow streets of the old town are slowly coming to life, zealous tourists are marching their sandals over the buckled cobblestones. He glances in the mirror before going out. Not a single crease – his collar is neatly ironed and his thick white hair impeccably combed. The fresh morning air helps soothe him. Dr Augusto pauses to catch his breath and wipe the sweat from his forehead – this climb will kill him one day. The coloured *sobrados* draw him on, and eventually he reaches the Square. The gentle sun caresses the faded walls of Father Denilson's church. As on every morning, the priest is cleaning, polishing and whistling. Freshly cut flowers sit on the steps, an offering from a believer. Pipoca snores on a bench, ink-stained hands crossed over his stomach. Dr Augusto waits patiently for the Father to finish decorating his church. As they do every Wednesday, Rubi and Safir have left a basket at the foot of the statue of Nossa Senhora de Aparecida: food for the boys for the coming week. The priest has added some old newspapers and patched clothes from the jumble sale. The Square takes care of its children.

Zé rubs away the traces by touch. The light bulb has been unscrewed. Only a murmur – a hardly audible, groaning death rattle – guides him. Scarlet rivulets flow into the veins of the ground, between the bare feet and the floppy bodies.

Zé rubs, on his knees. Full of rage and also despair. Drops of sweat fall from his forehead and into the purple pools. Next to him lies a man, his throat gaping with a slit so precise it could have been made by a surgeon. The Tuner's trademark: the virtuosity of his bow is unparalleled. The others surround the dead man while the crime is doctored. He must hurry, must finish before the arrival of the wardens, those scavengers whose silence is dearly bought. Zé rubs some more. His bony knees are grazed, and his ribs show through the beige cotton uniform. He thinks about Manuel, alone in Wing 5, the plague-ridden section. Zé works more fiercely. Manuel will get his bed in the sick bay. A man hoists himself up on someone's back and screws the light bulb back in. People start talking again. The stone has swallowed the blood: it feasts on the life that is draining away.

Father Denilson gives Dr Augusto a warm hug. The doctor has got that Wednesday look. Black rings deepen the bags under his always-anxious eyes. Despite his weariness, he gives off an irresistible strength, the gentle and resigned strength of those who have too often rubbed shoulders with suffering. As on every Wednesday, he is freshly shaven and smells of the French eau de cologne he loves so much. The priest gives him the basket with an encouraging smile. Rubi and Safir have surpassed themselves again, to the extent that the priest had to employ all his moral strength to stop himself tasting their prawn *moqueca*. Dr Augusto picks up the basket, surprised by its weight. Rubi and Safir will be feeding the whole prison! Quick, he's got to get a move on, the boys are waiting for him. Father Denilson accompanies him to the bus stop in silence, both men hoping that this Wednesday's visit will not be the last.

Rough hands run over his body. Greedy fingers with calloused skin bruise him, clasping hold of his skinny ankles. First the window and then the cell disappears from sight. Manuel never thought he would miss them, but he's afraid and he's cold. Zé can't do anything for him now. Manuel is heading alone to a certain death. The prisoners must have complained and shopped him to the chief warden – they are getting rid of the carcass to avoid contagion. He doesn't fight, half losing consciousness, overwhelmed by illness and by men. His body hasn't obeyed him for a long time now. It is tired, manhandled, dried out. This body that was taken so often, in that place behind the rocks, where the surf drowned out the groans of unknown men. Nights that repeated themselves endlessly, the moon their only witness. Harsh voices barking orders, then disappearing. Manuel can't bear it any more: he wants to leave, wants it to end. Only Zé keeps him back, giving him a little of that courage he has in spades. Suddenly: silence. The voices have quietened, the hands are no longer confining him. The suffocating stink of the cells has faded, a smell of ether is hanging in the air, the white walls are giving off a blinding light. Manuel slowly closes his eyes. His head is lying on a pillow now, and this comfort raises a weak smile. He's understood – it's the sick bay. Zé has done it. He can sleep.

The Tuner crosses the prison yard, one hand in the pocket of his black trousers. The others all have to wear the disturbingly bland beige uniform. Three men accompany him on his daily round. They stand at a respectful distance and wait for permission to speak. The Tuner reigns over Canju like Maria Aparecida used to reign over the Square. To each their kingdom. Thousands of eager eyes watch the king. Some bet on the length of his reign, some on the coming executions or the value of that week's drug traffic. His faithful lieutenant crouches in the corner, watching everything. Every one of Zé's senses is alert, lying in wait for the slightest hint of rumour or suspicious behaviour. Reigns tend to be short here. Boredom compounds tension, opening the way for murder, torture and rape, committed with indifference and sometimes even elation. Zé examines the faces. Beige death masks. The uniform has crept upwards: black, white, mixed or Indian, there's no colour here, only emptiness and absence. Zé scours the faces again and again. He's looking for the spark, the telling glimmer. The traitor. Nothing must happen to The Tuner. With a click of the fingers Zé is ordered to bring him his violin. Eyes dart about behind bars, and a frightened murmur runs through the building. The men cower in the backs of the cells or hide behind the piled-up bodies, at the risk of asphyxiation. Many bring a hand to their throats, dreading the lethal slit of the bow. Suddenly, a prolonged cry tears through the general dread. A solemn, harrowing note. The beginning of a Gypsy tune.

Osvaldinho, aka Soda, sets off on his rounds whistling the theme tune to *The Clone*. With his bucket, his broom and his knife he goes from floor to floor and wing to wing. A bit of mopping here, a bit of knifing there. It's important to keep things clean, so tough luck if a few get stabbed. He's just doing his job: housework. His instructions weren't more specific than that. Osvaldinho hates dirt and all the vermin that goes with it. He got that from his mother: the old girl was always disinfecting everything. Ever since he beat her to a pulp he's inherited all her obsessions. Whenever he sees rats or cockroaches, he screams. Nothing can calm him down. Well, almost nothing – there is one thing, and everyone in Canju knows what it is: a cold, fizzy Coke. The bubbles tickle his throat and help him forget the vile creatures. Even the wardens know about it – sometimes his screams interrupt a football match or a soap, so they always keep a Coke handy. The bosses of the eleven wings terrify the new boys with those screams, making out that someone is being tortured. It's one way of getting them in line. He hasn't been bumped off yet because he's the only one who can travel freely around the whole prison. He carries messages, phones and gossip when he's in his right mind. Often he forgets, but you just have to give him his Coke and it all comes flooding back. A Coke... Mmm... Just thinking about it gets him humming. Suddenly he remembers. That message for Wing

7 from the sick bay. Osvaldinho gets a move on. The Tuner mustn't be made to wait.

Gringa has deserted the church steps. Since Sergio's departure, she has retreated into a silence that no one has been able to break – she won't even listen to Pipoca's entreaties. Three kilos of hash deserves punishment – perhaps two years with no remission is a bit harsh, but that's life. Gringa looks ironically at Pipoca. Mama Lourdes was right, she is cursed. Sergio's trusting smile, Zé and Manuel's friendship. Lost. Lost. Lost. She pushes away their faces, she doesn't want to think of those children imprisoned inside ashy walls where the graffiti is scrawled in blood. Or of that smell. Indefinable. Sour, damp, rancid. Or of death on the prowl. Sergio. Far away, and alone too. She hadn't known. Gringa would like to cry. Zé and Manuel. She imagines what they must be going through, their terror. Two years without remission in that death-house where newcomers are sold at auction, fought over and then fucked like women. Gringa leans against the wall of Father Denilson's church. Her body slides down the stone, grazing itself, and collapses on the cobblestones. They are still a little warm, from the beautiful summer day.

Iemanja is wild today, her blue gown swells with fury. The small fishing boats pitch dangerously, hulls ready to dive into the deep arms of the raging waves. Dr Augusto feels giddy, as if he too is in danger of drowning. He looks over at the dunes instead. Miles of pale, gently oscillating sand. The wind blows against the windows, keeping away the first drops of rain. The ticket inspector walks up the bus to close them, but they are worn by the salt and sand and some get stuck, letting in the smell of the sea. Mothers, fiancées, children and pastors, they all gulp great breaths of the life-saving freshness. It dazes them, obliterating for a few seconds the decay of the prison and those who haunt it. Dr Augusto knows all the faces. Dona Sueli looks solemn – her two sons have been transferred, and no one could tell her where. Mariana's eyes are shining: today was the day for lovers' visits and she and Pedro were able to be with each other again. Senhor Joaquim's lips are set. He'll get off the bus without acknowledging the others, as he always does. This scorn is a poor disguise for his distress – his only son has become the Wing 3 whore. Dr Augusto doesn't see his own face, his own ravaged features. He would rather lose himself in the sadness of others.

The final notes resound in the yard, spreading and then slowly fading as they reach the cells. In tribute to this strange music not a single murmur breaks the silence. Soon the usual overwhelming clamour will return. The Tuner calmly returns his violin to its black leather case, enjoying this moment of absolute power. The wardens have gone back to their station for a last game of cards before the news. The guys can sort themselves out – and if something does happen, well, that will be one less criminal. An insistent splashing breaks the apparent tranquillity, a familiar sound that everyone knows: Osvaldinho with his broom and his bucket of bleach. The bucket of a thousand surprises – books, magazines, weapons, *maria louca* – whatever you want, it's there. All you have to do is sweet-talk Soda and pay his price. The lapping of bleach marks his progress as he walks slowly through the large room. Zé moves towards him: you've got to show your credentials before you can speak to the boss of Wing 7. He puts out his hand for Soda's unpredictable knife, but Soda ignores him and continues on his way. Zé stares intently at the tall, bowed body, soft as a piece of modelling clay – Osvaldinho's scruffy hair is the only remotely upright thing about him. He looks peaceful. Too peaceful. Zé feels his pulse quicken; he's about to do something bad. Zé rushes in front to block Soda's progress. The Tuner stands a few yards away observing the scene, unruffled, proud of his lieutenant's courage. Emaciated faces appear, pushing each other out of the way. They want to watch the show. Zé is in for it. Osvaldinho doesn't like obstacles, and nor does his knife. He looks up, shifting his weight from foot to foot, looking at Zé with his crazy eyes. They seem a little sad, regretful. Then, with one hand holding his equipment and the other in his pocket, he shoves Zé roughly aside and makes straight for The Tuner. Suddenly Zé understands. He throws himself desperately at Soda, trying to stop him from speaking. The broom handle falls to the ground and the bleach spills all over the yard, swallowing the old blotches of dried blood. But it's too late. Osvaldinho delivers his message. Manuel is dead.

The warmth of the cobblestones has evaporated, giving way to a dark, starless night. Gringa is asleep, huddled against the church wall. Tiny raindrops weave through cracks in the stone and splash on to her trousers. Her sleep is restless, she looks tense. Mama Lourdes stands watching her, the embers of her cigar moving dangerously close to the translucent skin she has always envied. She tests the slumped body with a deformed and fleshy foot. Not the slightest reaction. She derives a malicious pleasure from seeing the queen of the Square crashed out like a common beggar. The degeneration of others gives her a strange, almost sensual satisfaction. She fiddles with her cigar, smells it, takes a big drag and gleefully belches it into the face of Gringa, who coughs and opens an anxious eye. An incandescent flame shines in the night, dimly lighting up a massive, dark and terrifying shape. Gringa recoils, but her back is against the wall. A gravelly voice murmurs threats in her ear, intimations of new catastrophes. For the first time since Sergio left, Gringa's scream resounds through the Square.

Turco smiles. A woman is undressing him with her eyes while keeping watch on her child. Shamelessly. Arrogantly, even. A beautiful black woman with a taut, lithe body. Lovely enough to banish thoughts of Ivone and her green eyes. Wisps of hair protrude from her pink headscarf, accentuating the elegance of her features. The child is playing

quietly with a ball, a red ball with the paint peeling off it.
He's not interested in the adults' games. Turco wants her,
and this kid is a nuisance. His mother calls out firmly: it's
time to go home. She holds out her hand to the child. The
red ball lies on the floor, waiting to be picked up. The child
raises his eyes and sees Turco for the first time. He stares at
him and then turns to the ball. His mother leans down to
get it; so does Turco. He picks it up and puts it under his
arm. They can go home now. All three of them.

Zé is suffocating, face down on the floor. The bleach is burning his nostrils. He struggles, coughs and tries to get up, but
Osvaldinho holds him down firmly with the help of his
broom. Zé pushes at him with stick-like arms. The pressure
on the back of his neck intensifies: he can't breathe, the
bleach is knocking him out. People are whistling and making
fun of him. Osvaldinho is roaring with laughter: he thinks
it's hilarious. He turns his victim and works the broom over
his face, dunks it in the bleach and starts again. Zé needs a
good clean: he's got to forget Manuel and his perverted habits. Osvaldinho doesn't notice that the laughing has stopped,
that his shrill voice is the only sound in Wing 7. He takes
out his knife; he feels like sticking it in Zé's neck. Suddenly
he jumps. The Tuner is standing right in front of him, more
imposing than ever. He huddles into himself, not daring to
look up. The Tuner brings his bow to Osvaldinho's ear and
drags it slowly across his neck. Osvaldinho clings desperately
to his broom, panting. His knees give way, and suddenly
he's sloshing around in his bleach. The bow sinks in a bit
more, the strings stretched. He feels a drop of blood running
down his skin. He's about to yell out, but The Tuner is
pushing him towards the stairs. He crawls to the exit, the
grime sticking to his fingers – all he can think about is getting out of Wing 7 as fast as possible. The Tuner is squatting
at Zé's feet, murmuring quietly into his ear. His lieutenant
opens his eyes and looks at him for a long time, then holds
out his hand. The Tuner helps him up and gives him the

ceremonial embrace. His powerful body protects him, like a suit of armour. From now on, no one touches Zé.

Father Denilson doesn't know how to console Orphan Gabriela. He's never known what to say in cases of heart-break. That was more Ivone's department, but since she left for São Paulo most of her 'customers' are coming back to him. So from time to time he takes a furtive glance at women's magazines and notes bits of practical advice in his secret notebook, as well as some handy little phrases that sound full of wisdom, even if they don't actually mean much. He's tried them out in the confessional, and the results are promising. He's also had a look at a bit of feminist literature, but it seemed rather excessive. Father Denilson curses. He's mislaid his notebook – otherwise he could have had a sneaky look between two sobs and found something to soothe Gabriela. He doesn't know what to say. It's certainly not the time to talk about God and prayer. Perhaps he could try the Virgin Mary? She was a woman, after all. The priest plays with the beads of his rosary, rubbing each one hard. Nothing. His rosary doesn't yet have the same powers as Aladdin's lamp, and he can no longer count on Providence. Heavy footsteps reverberate in the nave, Orphan Gabriela stops crying. A shadow appears in the semi-darkness. Outside, the storm is rumbling. Father Denilson immediately recognises the slightly stooped profile and the well-cut suit. Dr Augusto is back. His head is bobbing gently, he doesn't have the strength to come any further, the basket of provisions falls from his hand and spills on to the floor. It is still half-full. Orphan Gabriela runs to Dr Augusto and helps him to pick up the provisions. Father Denilson is frozen, his limbs won't move. He stares at the Christ on the cross at the entrance to the church – his crown of thorns bruises the priest's own flesh. Dr Augusto is muttering, slumped on a pew. Gringa appears, distraught and dripping wet, and throws herself into the doctor's arms. Her eyes search out those of the priest, accusing him and his God. He shrinks back, overwhelmed by the hate in her eyes. She takes Dr Augusto's arm and leads him out of the church that was once a comfort to her.

Stiff. Cold. All that's left is Manuel's naked body laid out on a dirty sheet. Zé hides his tears in the curly brown hair. Manuel was so proud that it had finally grown back. The shearing on the first day had traumatised him for ages. Zé rests his hand on Manuel's forehead, slides it down to his still-open eyes. He gazes deep into them one last time and then strokes them shut, remembering their years of roaming and freedom. Zé must forget, must wipe it all out – otherwise he won't survive the horror that is Canju. The clock on the wall says six-thirty. Soon, they will come and get Manuel and chuck him into a hole in a wasteland adjoining Canju. An anonymous, shared grave. Promiscuity even in death. Zé won't have it. Manuel will have his own beautiful tombstone engraved with gold letters and a photo, like in the movies. And flowers. Fresh. Not those artificial ones that fade with time. Flowers like in Father Denilson's church, vivid and fragrant. Zé will find the money. Manuel will have his tombstone – the only thing he'll ever have.

Gringa has dressed in black. Her hair is contained in a lace mantilla, her eyes are overflowing with grief and bitterness. The Square's Madonna is on her way, an alabaster statue crumbling under adversity. She waves wearily to Dr Augusto, Pipoca, the priest and the others before getting into the taxi. The Square is behind her, then Pelourinho. Away from their kindly concern, Gringa collapses. Her hands are frozen, and her courage is weakening with each passing minute. The taxi driver no longer dares to look in the rear-view mirror: her silent tears are distracting him – he swears never to accept a job to Canju again. It's always the same: a journey that puts him on a downer for the rest of the week. To hell with the money: from now on he'll only take on little jobs within the city. The customer speaks for the first time. Her voice is solemn, shattered. She hurries him, asks him to speed up – the gates of the prison will close in a few hours, she has to get there as soon as possible. Her head is buzzing with images: being searched, meeting the director, the long corridors, the clanking of keys, the insults and threats from wardens and inmates. And most of all, the smell. Gringa is already suffocating. She remembers Sergio with Zé and Manuel on the Square. They were such a threesome. They really loved each other. She won't leave without Zé and Manuel. This time, she won't leave them alone. The children of the Square must come home. Everyone is making the church ready for the final reunion. Gringa clutches her camera to her chest: at the slightest protest she'll shoot hundreds of pictures and expose Canju as the worst penal colony in South America. The press loves those sordid stories. The taxi comes to a stop – they've arrived. Gringa is ready. The Tuner is waiting for her.

Osvaldinho left Wing 7 at top speed. He has gone back to his rounds, obeying a summons to Wing 5. What a day. He's dreading this interview in the stronghold of Commando Vermelho, the faction feared by prisoners, management and politicians alike. But at Canju, the CV has failed. The Tuner is the undisputed boss – well, almost. There is the terrifying Pimentao, boss of Wing 5, a small wing near the cemetery. Gossip has it this is because Wing 5 has direct access, so they can bury their dead without any waste of time. Osvaldinho heads to the meeting with a heavy step. Even his bleach is quiet at the bottom of the bucket. His pliable body is looking more and more floppy, his quiff has collapsed. He takes his time climbing the stairs. Fat blue flies are fighting over the fruit rotting on every step. He shivers. Pot-bellied flies, gorging on filth. He can hardly help himself: his broom is itching to work, the tip of his knife can't wait to pierce their bloated flesh. But Pimentao is waiting for him on the top floor of his prison suite, surrounded by lackeys. He has got wind of Manuel's death and Zé's promotion. Osvaldinho never likes coming here, least of all today. He is not happy with this summons. He has always been able to maintain a certain neutrality, but this time Pimentao won't let him slip away. He'll want to know everything – he will want Zé's head. Osvaldinho doesn't yet know how to refuse.

Turco gets into the green Coccinelle without a word. It's an ancient, methane-fuelled car covered in stickers – 'Baby on Board', 'Jesus Loves You'. The child is sitting in the back with the ball on his knees, humming away and drawing on the misted-up windows. Turco lets himself be led by this strong, calm woman. Her short, unpolished nails put his mind at ease. She changes gear with an air of determination, now and then re-tuning the radio to avoid the adverts. The Coccinelle drives away from Salvador centre, the tarmac giving way to a beaten-earth road lined with houses made of any and every substance to hand, and banana plantations scattered here and there. Scruffy-looking kids follow the car on their makeshift bicycles. The child waves cheerfully at them, watching as they fall behind in a cloud of dust. The radio crackles, the singer's voice breaks up and dies. The child has dozed off, curled up against a bag of dirty laundry. The ball has slipped out of his hands. The mother looks at him lovingly for a moment, shifts into neutral and puts her hand on Turco's thigh. She parks the car on the verge – the house isn't much further but never mind.

Manuel's *toilette* is finished: he looks better now in this suit, with his hair combed. And he smells good, thanks to the eau de cologne Dr Augusto gave them last Wednesday. Zé is satisfied. If he'd had some make-up he could have worked miracles. Manuel was worn to the bone – Canju broke and destroyed him. Sure, it was the disease and the lack of medication too. But fear was the straw that broke his back. Insidious and slimy, fear kills with total impunity. Not a day passes without a victim. Fear is the perfect accountant, with its daily quota of deaths. It kills those that don't stand up to it. Manuel wasn't able to pretend, to put on the lifeless mask, the lacklustre expression, to feign life-saving indifference. Manuel is the day's quarry – tomorrow there will be others. And every day. Zé gently shuts the door of the sick bay: he hates leaving him alone in this dark room without a single candle to keep vigil. He makes his way to Wing 7 to let The Tuner know that Manuel is ready to go, but Osvaldinho and Pimentao's flunkeys are blocking his way. They take him to Wing 5 where their boss is waiting.

The Tuner rests his violin gently on his knees. The visiting room is empty, the guards have evaporated. Gringa will be here in a moment – she's in the director's office pleading for the two kids, not knowing that the final decision is his. Manuel can go, his corpse is no use to anyone here. But not Zé: he's a child of the Square, loyal to the bone. Outside he has no future. Here, one day he'll take over. Take over from him. Only a few months of Zé's sentence remain, but The Tuner will find a way to keep him here. He'll blame his next murder on him. He plucks the strings of his violin, the bow waiting impatiently on a chair. The Tuner hasn't seen Gringa since Maria Aparecida disappeared, since that tragic night when he fled Salvador. He can still remember an indescribably sweet look, without which she would never have escaped with her life. One of his men knocks on the door, and Gringa appears. He stands to greet her. She shakes his hand but pulls away quickly, as if his touch frightened her. She has changed: her eyes are veiled and her face closed, and she moves uncertainly. The Tuner is disappointed. He had thought she was invulnerable, confident. His fingers drum on the table; the visiting room suddenly seems tiny, stifling. He's got to leave, got to get back to his yard and the open air. She senses his sullen mood, so she puts a hand on his. The Tuner is overcome by this show of tenderness. He's listening.

Pimentao has a nasty reputation at Canju, which he feeds with a certain glee and not much effort. Cruelty comes naturally to him: he likes to say it's a gift from the gods. For several months now, his reputation has been suffering from competition with The Tuner and his precision strings, his elegant methods of killing. And he has to make do with decrepit old Wing 5, sandwiched between the cemetery and the linen department. Pimentao can't stand the humiliation and is constantly plotting his revenge. Besides, he's having fun right now, with Zé as his hostage. If this poof doesn't bring him The Tuner by nightfall, his stiff of a Manuel will go to the dogs. Osvaldinho leans against the wall watching Zé. The boy doesn't move, but his eyes are spitting hate. There's nothing left of the morning's terrified kid. The Tuner has chosen his heir well.

Dinora hangs up the washing with quick, efficient movements. She's still got two machines to do and thirty-three uniforms to iron before the evening's delivery. She'd like to make the most of Turco's body again tonight. She'll have to get a move on and put the kid to bed early. Turco is dozing in the garden with half an eye on Dinora's hips as she picks up her washing. She passes in front of him carrying a big hamper full of beige uniforms. He can't quite make out the black letters on the back – probably one of those French supermarkets. Dinora sets up her ironing board and works diligently. Turco stands up to put his arms around her. She smells good, squeaky clean. He can read the letters easily now, over her shoulder: *Canju, Federal Prison*. He moves away from Dinora, back to his place in the sun. He had forgotten about Zé and Manuel.

Osvaldinho carefully examines the can that Pimentao tossed him as payment. It's a small, warm, sticky can with rusty rims. It must come from the director's storehouse, that little room to which no one has access. But Osvaldinho knows exactly what goes on in there – every time he goes near, it's party time. Rats and cockroaches having a hoot making their deafening racket. He imagines the rats running about among the sacks of rice and black beans, their hooked claws sliding on the plastic-wrapped cans of fizzy drinks. His breathing speeds up, the scream is about to burst out, but it dies in his throat. Osvaldinho is furious. Pimentao has taken the piss out of him. This is not Coke at all – it's Pepsi. A bland and over-sweet substitute. An unforgivable offence. One single can of this bloody Pepsi, and it's dirty. He deserved at least two cases of Coca-Cola. New, wrapped in plastic. That's enough humiliation for one day. It's time to settle the score. With his broom, and his bucket full to the brim, Osvaldinho feels on top form. Time to do some real cleaning...

Gringa takes a sip of water. The interview is over, and The Tuner has gone back to his lair to organise Manuel's departure. As for Zé, he wouldn't hear of it. She tried everything, but he was totally indifferent to her arguments – Zé would not leave Canju. The door opens, and the wardens take up their posts again for the last hour of visitors. A woman comes in and greets the screws one by one; she seems to know them well. She carries a hamper in her arms which no one searches. She walks nonchalantly over to the far end of the room. Her pink headscarf contrasts with her dark skin and with Gringa's pallor. The two women check each other out, without animosity. Dinora sits down and smoothes the pleats in her dress as she glances discreetly at the unknown woman. Pimentao arrives and whistles at Gringa under the knowing eyes of the wardens. Dinora smells danger: she steps forward and takes her husband's arm, leading him away from the woman. Pimentao keeps looking back at her. Must be the violinist's new conquest.

Zé looks in the mirror and doesn't recognise himself. His features are fading: fear is taking over, the beige mask is gaining ground. He brings his hands to his face: he wants to rip off this thick waxy layer; someone else can have it. Zé won't give in. He turns on the tap and splashes himself with icy water. The signs are still there. He turns off the cold and lets the tap run until it's boiling before dunking his face. His skin is burning, the pain is unbearable, but he bears it. Zé would like to forget about Pimentao's orders, but he can't abandon Manuel. Not now. He'll betray The Tuner, but he'll never give him over to Pimentao – he'll kill him instead. Zé looks in the mirror again. He is back.

The air caresses the pale wood of the violin, making the strings vibrate and emit contented little sighs. The Tuner pricks up his ears – they don't sound right, too shrill. Wing 7: the light bulbs start their nocturnal comings and goings as the men return to their cells one by one, in pre-established order. The most powerless will go to the end, next to the urinals. The more privileged will be able to lie down on the ground near the yard. Some try to negotiate a few hours sleep or a place near the television. The Tuner looks for Zé. He frowns – the kid isn't at his station. For the first time. This absence is a very bad sign. He settles his chair in the middle of the yard and waits for the gossip to come to him. Eventually it trails in, bucket in one hand and dignity in the other. Osvaldinho has come to ask forgiveness and to warn him about the danger he is in. The Tuner listens, imperturbable. Osvaldinho leaves happy: The Tuner has given him permission to clean Wing 5.

Turco watches the child distractedly. The boy won't go to sleep. He's playing with his ball and doesn't want his company. Dinora has left them here while she goes to drop the washing at Canju; she's promised to be back before sunset. Turco turns on the TV. He thinks he sees Ivone, but his eyes are playing tricks on him. Boredom is starting to get the better of him; he won't last long here. A dodgy reception makes the image all fuzzy, which is enough to drive him mad – he turns it off and wanders round the little house. The boy runs up and drags him off to the kitchen: he's hungry. Confused, Turco looks at him without knowing what he means. The child doesn't get upset; he just asks again for something to eat, a hint of exasperation in his voice. Turco opens the fridge and gets out milk and sliced bread. The child waits patiently for him to finish. Turco looks for jam but can't find any. The cupboards are crammed full of airtight jars. He opens one. Inside are transparent plastic bags stuffed with white powder. The sort of thing Zé and Manuel used to sell some nights when times were hard, and the reason they've been sent to Canju. Turco slams the cupboard shut and takes the child by the hand. They're going to find his mama in the prison. Supper will have to wait.

Gringa is arguing with the chief warden. The doors are about to close, she can't wait for The Tuner any longer: she's got to collect Manuel. The warden refuses, categorically: he can't do that without the agreement of his superiors. She might have more luck tomorrow, with the director. 'The inmates don't make the rules at Canju,' he bellows, 'whatever it might look like.' Gringa loses her cool and shoves him aside to get through the visiting-room door. No one will stop her leaving with Manuel. Pimentao watches with amusement. As for Dinora, she no longer looks so nonchalant: this unknown woman is about to create a scene. Her husband stands up quickly and walks over to Gringa, ever so friendly. Smiling and swaggering, he offers to escort her safely to the sick bay. Gringa shrinks back, suspicious of this sudden kindness. The woman in the pink headscarf looks haggard – she thinks she can detect jealousy in her gaze and turns away. With her camera firmly in hand, she walks towards Pimentao. The chief warden lets them go without a word – he's too busy counting his cash. At Canju, the rules change very fast.

Hands reach out through the bars of the cells. As he walks down the corridor the guards greet him and congratulate him on his promotion, a note of fear in their voices. Zé goes down to the ground floor, where his boss is waiting for him in the yard. He has slipped a dagger into his sock. With a knife his chances are poor, but he hasn't managed to find a gun in such a short space of time. He will never hand The Tuner over to Pimentao alive. The fear has left his face: he arrives in the yard escorted by an invisible army. A nostalgic tune welcomes him. Low-pitched, strained chords. The Tuner is playing to a full house tonight. He is facing his audience, with his back to the entrance of Wing 7, at the mercy of Zé and his dagger.

The Square is getting ready for its child's funeral. Rubi and Safir replace the puny old candles with tall colourful ones, while Sonia the pro, assisted by Orphan Gabriela, arranges the flowers. Pipoca walks through the pews putting out song sheets. He has taken his mission seriously and is using the opportunity to practise the hymns. Dr Augusto has taken refuge in the sacristy to write something in honour of the deceased, but his grief prevents him from concentrating. The others are waiting reverently for Gringa to arrive with the boys. A fresh breeze is blowing through the Square, and the first stars are appearing in the sorrowful sky. The priest crosses the chancel to join the doctor. He has come to collect his alb and any news. No sign of Gringa, but they're not too worried: the formalities must have taken a while, they won't be long now. A man knocks timidly at the door. He is nervously turning a straw hat in his knotty fingers and barely dares to look at them. The priest urges him to speak. The man is a taxi driver – he took their friend to Canju, but the prison gates shut before she came back out. The wardens advised him to leave if he didn't want to spend the night outdoors, on the other side of the wall. Frightened by these threats he sped back to Salvador, and now his conscience is bothering him. If one of them would accompany him, he might find the courage to return to Canju.

Pimentao's grim stare skates over Gringa, who does her best to hide her disgust. He has put his chubby hand around her waist and taken her to visit Wing 5 while Manuel's corpse is being prepared. He is proud to show off his seduction of the violinist's lady-love to his men. She came with the real boss, with no recourse to weapons or threats. The servile prisoners clap, but all Pimentao hears are the howls of his rival: he imagines him beseeching, at his mercy. Gringa moves imperceptibly away from her jailor in search of some air, a window. The suffocating smell of the building is choking her, seeping into every pore, clinging to her skin. She knows she has been trapped, but it's too late for regrets now: flattery is her only chance. An article on the biggest trafficker in Bahia. He listens with interest, seduced by the idea. They will go up to his quarters: top floor of Wing 5, with a view of the cemetery from above, perfect for her photos. The press coverage will assure his reputation beyond these walls. Coarse laughs accompany their journey. In the shadowy half-light, Gringa steps in a puddle. Her nostrils burn with the smell of bleach. Short of breath, Pimentao clambers up the stairs without noticing either how clean they are or Osvaldinho, who has melted into the darkness.

Turco speeds through the banana fields on the neighbour's moped. He is going to Canju to give the kid back to his mother before leaving Bahia. Perhaps he'll join Ivone in São Paulo. Lightning illuminates the beaten-earth road and makes the child behind him shiver. Small fingers grip his T-shirt. The child's head is huddled against his back, his little heart beating violently and spasmodically, unbelievably strong for such a small kid. Turco is moved and squeezes his hand in reassurance. A road sign indicates that they are now close to the federal prison. The boy guides him to the entrance of Wing 5, confessing proudly that he knows this place well: his mother brings him once a month to visit his dad, the famous Pimentao. Turco hides his surprise and curses his misfortune. They are blinded by circles of cold, interrogatory white light. The watchtower probes them with its powerful rays. The child moves close to him again, in search of a little warmth. A bus full of sadness passes by on the other side of the road. The driver advises him to turn around: today's visiting hours are over. Turco parks the moped near the prison and walks towards the heavy, grey metal door. A man with an all-powerful sub-machine gun repels them back towards the parking lot. Turco points at the child and says that Pimentao is waiting for them inside. The kid proudly repeats the name of his father. The man shouts into his walkie-talkie and then lets them through. Turco and Pimentinha walk in, hand in hand.

A deep, clean stab in the jugular: Zé mustn't hesitate any longer. So what if he's attacking from behind, so what if it's dishonourable? With his violin to his chin, The Tuner has mentally risen above the courtyard, unconcerned with death waiting motionless behind him. The notes break out one by one, scattering in the yard – Canju and Wing 7 no longer exist. Zé doesn't move, unable to slip his hand into the sock where he has hidden his knife. He is paralysed. He thinks of Manuel, alone in the sick bay; he longs to be back with him. He grabs the dagger, rubs the freezing blade against his fist and brandishes it at his boss. The notes choke and die. The dagger and the bow clatter to the floor. The blood of the child of the Square spills over the courtyard.

Osvaldinho slaps at his bleach with a long, floppy hand. It is splashing too noisily in his new bucket: its lapping will end up alerting this vermin Pimentao. He can hear him flaunting his power and mocking The Tuner's declining empire. Osvaldinho's senses are on the alert: the putrid sweat is coming closer, revolting his sensitive nostrils. A woman is following the Wing 5 boss. She is peering into the darkness, aware of a hidden presence. Her frightened body brushes past him. Pimentao sends his lackeys down to the floors below to make sure that no one comes into his suite: nobody must interrupt his photo shoot with Gringa. Osvaldinho slips in behind the couple. The woman keeps glancing back, reassured by the discreet presence that she takes to be The

Tuner. Eyes shining with lust, Pimentao goes over to her, claiming his dues. Osvaldinho is quick to recognise the vicious glint in his eye, exactly like that of a starving rat. He can't stand those squalid beasts, those greedy, mean rodents. He remembers the small rusty can of Pepsi. He pushes Gringa out of the way – it's time to get rid of this dirty beast, time to kill it, to reduce it to nothing, to neutralise it once and for all. The scream rises in his throat and explodes through Wing 5. The knife thrusts: once, twice, ten times. Pimentao's shapeless bulk collapses. Osvaldinho tips his bleach over the corpse. Now that the cleaning is finished, he needs a Coke. Ice-cold.

The hamper is heavy this evening. Dinora can't stop thinking about Gringa, about Pimentao and his cruel games. Messenger, linen-maid, carrier pigeon – they are all lies to cover up what she's become over time. A dealer. The most efficient in the whole state of Bahia, boasts Pimentao. He is proud of all the ideas she comes up with for hiding the gear. The only reason Dinora has been so ingenious is to protect her son. She wants to get back to him. The chief warden calls her over. He's lost his friendly smile and looks down at her contemptuously. She'd better pick up her kid quickly and get out of here, he says – Pimentao has got himself killed, there's nothing left for her here. Dinora runs to her child, the hamper of uniforms falls to the ground, the packets of white powder scatter on the visiting-room floor. Turco passes the child to his mother and looks away. He's got nothing to do with this woman and her trafficking – he's come for Zé and Manuel. The chief warden bursts into a cruel laugh. If the gentleman would like to follow him to the morgue . . .

The Tuner picks up his bow. The string has broken. Zé fought right to the end, his resolute and fearless eyes looking deep into his own. His dagger shines in the semi-darkness, next to his lifeless arm. The Tuner can't drag his eyes from the ground. He grabs his young lieutenant's weapon. The dagger weighs barely a few ounces – it's as light as a child's toy. He slips it into his belt, picks up the bow from the chair with utter disgust and snaps it.

The taxi driver swears this is the last time a woman or a priest will get the better of him with their pleas. He's already been waiting for more than an hour, and his customers still haven't come out of the prison. At this rate he'll be taking the inmates as fares. At last the heavy prison gates swing open. The sight is stunning, heavenly even. A mass of pale wax candles lights up the windows of all eleven wings. Their flickering flames accompany two caskets towards the exit and illuminate the black flags flying proudly from the prison bars. Gringa is leading the cortège, Father Denilson and Turco follow behind the rough wooden caskets that some cellmates insisted on carrying. The taxi-cum-hearse carries them silently to Salvador. From the roof of Wing 7, The Tuner's dark gaze follows the children of the Square until the red tail lights disappear into the darkness. Then, with a wave of his hand, he gives the sign. The candles go out one by one, swallowed by the night. Canju fades away. Only Zé's candle, in cell 402, survives. The beige wax melts, sliding down the stone, slithering through the bricks and finally sinking into the earth. The Tuner cups the flame in his hand to resuscitate it one last time before it, too, dies. He brings his violin up to the candle. The flame encircles the instrument and devours it, the wood spluttering, then flaring up. The ashes are carried on the wind, far away, towards Iemanja, queen of the sea. All that's left is the echo of a Gypsy tune.

The carved wooden door is wide open, and joyful hymns ring out. It's time for a party. The Square is meeting its children for one last celebration. A gleaming walkway of orchids, roses, arums and white lilies greets Zé and Manuel. The moon shines through the stained-glass windows, its multicoloured rays sparkling on the faded walls. Gringa brings up the rear of the procession, enveloped in her black lace mantilla. She walks slowly up the church steps. The wind buffets her, but with a final effort she makes it into the nave. The church is packed – she doesn't acknowledge anyone. Not Orphan Gabriela, not Pipoca, not Rubi, whose joy has vanished. Maria Aparecida is waiting for her at the foot of the altar, majestic, dressed in white. Gringa lifts up her black veil; it falls among the petals. She is imprisoned in a bittersweet fragrance and encircled by drums. Gringa goes into a trance, choked by an unknown force. Maria Aparecida lays a wrinkled hand on her eyelids, heavy with tears, and wipes clean the traces of that April morning of another life, far away.

My name is Maria Aparecida, queen of Bahia, adored by all. I wash my hands as often as I can – it's not an obsession but a way of sloughing off the despair that I have begotten. I pretended to be mad so as to forget his child's eyes, begging for a love I could not give. I sacrificed my son for fame and for men. Iemanja would not take his sadness, so, to punish me, he murdered the joy in others. Forgive me, O goddess of the sea, and save my son from his torments, wash his crimes clean and drown me in your spray.